Sagan, Françoise

A fleeting sorrow

A FLEETING SORROW

A
FLEETING
SORROW

FRANÇOISE
SAGAN

TRANSLATED BY RICHARD SEAVER

ARCADE PUBLISHING • NEW YORK

First English-language Edition

Originally published in France under the title *Un chagrin de passage*

The characters and events in this book are fictitious. Any similarity to
real persons, living or dead, is coincidental and not intended by the
author.

Library of Congress Cataloging-in-Publication Data

Sagan, Françoise, 1935–
    [Chagrin de passage. English]
    A fleeting sorrow / Françoise Sagan; translated from the
French by Richard Seaver. — 1st English language ed.
        p.   cm.
    ISBN 1-55970-308-3
    I. Seaver, Richard. II. Title
PQ2633.U74C4713   1995
843'.914 — dc20   95-17751

Published in the United States by Arcade Publishing, Inc., New York

Distributed by Little, Brown and Company

10   9   8   7   6   5   4   3   2   1

BP

PRINTED IN THE UNITED STATES OF AMERICA

For Felix and Ingrid Mechoulam

I

I TAKE IT YOU'VE BEEN SMOKING for a long time?"

"I'm a smoker," Paul corrected, refusing to disown by a miserable change of tense a habit that was as ingrained in him as it was pleasurable — even if it were to cost him his life. That this detestable little doctor had just had the gall to inform him that he had only a short time to live was already bad enough. He had no intention of adding insult to injury by demeaning his old friend, "tobacco."

Aside from his initial confusion, Paul had also had to overcome his irritation, that same irritation he always felt about those who were the bearers of bad tidings. But little by little his impending death struck him as completely plausible. . . . Something about the place itself, this tasteless, anonymous doctor's office, the muffled sounds drifting up from the street below, something about both the normality and banality of this scene — perhaps even more than the word "cancer" that had just emerged from the doctor's mouth — seemed to belie the catastrophe.

"It goes without saying you should get a second opinion," said the little doctor, who was his own doctor's replacement. As he looked at him, Paul decided that one of his forebears had to be a hamster. "You should see some specialists, obviously," the doctor went on. "This is the kind of news that clearly calls for confirmation. Although, in your case, I fear all the tests came back . . ." The doctor's voice trailed off. And Paul cursed himself for being so stupid as to have his annual physical not with his own doctor but with this cretin of a replacement.

The doctor picked up and held aloft the X-rays of Paul's lungs — these missile photographs, this tarot pack of death — with a kind of careful consideration, even esteem, for the strength, the efficiency, the proof positive of "our" cancer, as he described it! No . . . it was just too goddamn much! The doctor's gloomy admiration for the medical proof he was brandishing was something his patient could simply not appreciate or share. The man should have understood that, for God's sake! How in the world could he, Paul, have managed to stumble on such a total fool to deliver the most important message he had ever received? "For the fact is, I'm going to die. In six months I'll be dead, gone, no longer here," he kept saying to himself over and over again. What surprised him most was that he didn't *feel* anything, and he would repeat the sentences in his head, interjecting now and then a mixture of disbelief and fear, the way one gingerly touches the area around a newly opened wound to see if it hurts. "In six months, nothing! I won't feel a thing! I won't be here . . . me . . . Paul! . . ."

And suddenly the reality of death struck him full force, as if he had been hit in the head, and he doubled over on his chair, his mind suddenly flooding with a very clear, precise memory. It was an afternoon two or three years ago at the Evry racetrack. He'd been down at the paddock, and so engrossed in his racing form that he was paying no attention to the horses parading past him either on their way to the starting gate or to be weighed in, when all of a sudden something terrifying had literally burst through the racing form and grazed his forehead. Instinctively he had jerked his head back. One of the passing horses had kicked up its heels, and one of its hooves had missed him by a fraction of an inch. He had seen the deadly object — iron and hoof and hair — zoom to eye level, then fall back. To his surprise and shame, it had taken Paul a full minute to recover, to stop trembling. And it was that experience that had enabled him to seize, to understand the full impact of, the doctor's diagnosis: Paul wanted to pull back, jerk his head away, as if, once again, to parry the mortal blow. But this time he could not. This time he knew there was no way out. No second chance.

He must have turned pale, because the hamster — yes, Paul decided, the man, with his tiny eyes and pouchy cheeks, did look just like a hamster — was leaning over him with what seemed to Paul an expression of sadistic satisfaction. Yet Paul's heartbeat was back to normal; he found it possible to breathe again. The horror of the preceding second faded into the background, but he had brushed up against the terror, the full horror of the thing, the unbearable notion. And he was amazed by his reaction. For the first time he understood the lies, the refusals to accept the evidence, that he had so often witnessed among his friends and acquaintances. The dying who looked forward to the future with confidence . . . The people under sentence of death who filled their minds with projects down the road . . . The very "idea" was unbearable. Period. And tomorrow no doubt, the day after tomorrow, very soon in any event, he knew that he too would find a way to turn his back on reality, deny the evidence of his death, refuse to accept the death notice he had just been handed.

"You're not feeling well? Or is it that you find me too forthright, too plainspoken? I'm afraid I belong to the school of medicine that believes it's best to tell patients the truth, the whole truth. . . . At least adults."

To make matters worse, for God's sake, this medical midget considers himself an adult! Did he think Paul was an adult as well? How could he be an adult when all he wanted was to be eleven years old again, to rush into the room of his parents — both dead, unfortunately — and beg for their help? They were the only ones who could tell him not to pay any attention to what the silly doctor had said, to reassure him that it was utter nonsense, that everything was going to be all right. They alone could have turned his world right side up again, sent him back to his bedroom completely reassured, that adolescent bedroom where nobody ever died. Later on, Paul would reproach himself for having first thought of his dear, departed parents rather than of the women in his life, who were alive and well. But when he thought about it, that instinctive choice did not really surprise him all that much. He had always known how strong his ties to childhood were, much stronger in fact than those he had forged as an adult.

And once again he had seen the proof of that basic truth: only his parents would have found it scandalous, totally unacceptable, that their son should die of cancer at age forty. The rest of the world would find it normal. The way of the world. The luck of the draw. His friends and relations were going to find it sad, even very sad, a pity, most unfortunate, or stupid. But no one would think about his death the way he and his parents would: unthinkable.

"My colleagues may have other opinions about how long you have," the doctor was going on. "I gave you six months. I could have said three months, or nine months, or a month. . . ."

"It doesn't matter —" Paul said mechanically.

But the doctor cut him off. "Don't say that! Today that may strike you as unimportant, since we're not talking about something that's going to happen tomorrow. But believe me, six months from now you'll thank me for each extra day you live beyond that date! And by the same token, you'll curse me if you fall short of those six months, even by a single day. Just wait. You'll see. . . ."

And, in fact, Paul envisioned that long line of men who had tried to put up a good front in the face of this medical cretin's prognostications, and who, coming up to the end of their six months' term, had begged whatever god was theirs to grant them just three days more, three days of unholy torture, no doubt, as the doctor had promised. There was something so smug about the doctor's tone — spiced with disdain — that Paul suddenly stood up. How he hated the man! But then he sat back down. This man was the only one who knew the truth, the only person who all of a sudden was not an outsider, the only person who knew the real Paul as he was now: a survivor, yes, but relegated now to death row. Another man altogether, he would later describe it. To whom could he tell the truth? To whom did he have to lie? He didn't know. All he knew was that in the presence of this man he despised he had to keep cool, remain calm, do or say nothing he would later regret. It was a simple matter of self-respect, a stupid, middle-class reaction that he wished he could eliminate . . . but at least it had the virtue of giving him courage, or the semblance of courage.

Dr. Moron had seemed relieved when Paul had first gotten to his feet, then disappointed when he had sat back down. So Paul made up his mind to stay there, to saddle the doctor with his presence as long as possible, even force him to engage in small talk if he could.

"Do you plan to travel?"

"Excuse me? No, I don't think so."

Paul was surprised. The very idea struck him as ridiculous. In the past — even as recently as this morning — he had thought about traveling to distant places, of seeing foreign landscapes and visiting cities he had till now only dreamed of. The Middle East,

Asia, cities by the sea, and mountain vistas that had, in times past, filled his mind and fired his imagination. But henceforth they would be nothing more than sites he would never see or to which he would never return. He was painfully aware that from now on these would be for him nothing more than places he'd regret never having seen. No longer oceans to swim in but oceans he would never see or hear again. What till today he had thought of as future possible discoveries were, as of this moment, gone, finished, wiped out. All future projects, every attractive and charming possibility, now had to be thought of as separations, like toys you'd been given that — you were now told — would have to be returned to the store. . . . Too soon! Nothing on this good earth belonged to him anymore, this earth that was his, that he so obviously loved and enjoyed. There were so many people who did not love life, who did not appreciate being here. Why him, of all people, him who loved life to the hilt? Why had this happened to him? For God's sake, he wasn't even forty! He wouldn't even be granted forty years to taste all the worldly pleasures he had dreamed of. . . . It was too unfair. (Now wait a minute, his mind cautioned: what about all the terrible catastrophes that occur every day on good old planet earth, all the indescribable atrocities, what about *that* injustice, especially when it involves women and children? Keep your sense of proportion.)

"I'll dictate a letter to Dr. Barondess," the hamster was going on from somewhere very far away. "He's the best in the business. Of course you may want to consult another expert of your choice. But I highly recommend Barondess. In my view there's no one more qualified. I'll have my nurse type up the letter immediately. Oh . . . I forgot, she's not in today," he said. "In any case, I'll get the letter to you tomorrow."

Ah, yes, his nurse, the lovely creature who had been the recent object of Paul's persistent pursuit, was indeed not in today. Paul had noticed her absence as soon as he had set foot in the waiting room. He had launched an all-out assault on the beautiful but doubtless shallow and hopefully shameless young thing, to whom Paul suspected the hamster owed a fair portion of his patients. Paul for one. They had a date for tea next Tuesday, and the intentions of the "tea" were unequivocal. The doctor seemed embarrassed to announce that his nurse wasn't in today, and suddenly everything became clear to Paul. Of course, there was a correlation between her absence and his "sickness." He wasn't contagious, but he might just as well have been. It wasn't all that simple. Desire, even the basest kind, required the notion of futurity if it was ever to come off. A man without a future, a dying man, was no longer desirable. And however stupid such a reaction might have seemed, Paul knew that if the situation was ever reversed, he would feel the same way about the woman. Desire would have turned into compassion. Which is tantamount to saying that desire would vanish into thin air. He would have to hide the truth of his situation as long as possible from the women he might want to seduce. There was no way he would be able to bear that look of pity

he was certain he'd detect in their eyes, as he'd be incapable of dealing with the inevitable questions they'd
ask in place of the simple yeses and nos of a normal
relationship.

But six months? What did six months really mean?
A brief moment in time or an eternity? The very notion that this strong body, this blood coursing with
desire, this healthy physical specimen was going to
desert him, was without warning and the slightest
sign of betrayal going to turn into his enemy — or
rather the lair of his enemy — this notion struck him
as even more depressing than anything else. He
glanced quickly at his hand, and imagined it an object
of disgust or pity, which it may already have become
to the buxom nurse. And suddenly he felt sick to his
stomach. What bothered him most was the banality
of the whole thing. He had always known that he was
going to die someday. He also knew that every year a
certain percentage — he couldn't remember the number exactly — of men in his age group died of cancer.
All right, as of today I've become a statistic, part of
that statistic. As simple as that. Nothing out of the ordinary, nothing very surprising or remarkable. Hap-
pens every day. And he, Paul, who would have been
more than willing to die behind the wheel, to become
part of the equally bad — and probably worse — statistic of automobile accidents, had no say in the matter. Except for the fact that the "matter" of which he
was now a vital statistic was simply unbearable to
him. His death would come as a shock to him and him
alone, he kept thinking. People would be surprised by

it, those who loved him would surely grieve. But his death would not *shock* anyone the way today's news had shocked him. He felt rejected, ridiculed, debased. Yes, debased; that was the word.

For the moment that was all he was asking: that the experience of the flashing metal horseshoe that had appeared out of nowhere and shattered his racing form not repeat itself. He could not go through another near death and then return to life as if nothing had happened. The next few weeks were going to be a nightmare. "Actually," he said to himself, "I don't mind dying. I just don't want to dwell on it. I don't want to be like all those people I've known through the years who, knowing they're about to die, go into complete denial. That has always amazed me. And disappointed me." For Paul, who considered himself to be among the most tolerant of men — or at least among the most indulgent — had often been upset and, yes, disappointed by how poorly his friends had dealt with death. And yet within a week he, Paul, would doubtless find a way to circumvent the truth, since the truth was untenable. He'd tell people he had tuberculosis, God knows what, some disease that might be curable. That's what everyone else did, to avoid facing the truth. And Paul would end up doing the same thing everyone else did.

The hamster had closed the door behind him without Paul's ever having laid eyes on the beautiful nurse. All he had seen was her red scarf hanging on the coatrack, perhaps forgotten in her haste to leave the previous evening. It was dark on the landing outside the

doctor's office, and Paul stood there for a moment
without moving, his hand gripping the railing. Then
he started downstairs with the same sprightly step
he'd picked up in high school, skipping rather than
walking: one, two, three; one, two, three; one, two,
three . . . Noisily, angrily. Here the noise was muffled
by the stairway carpet, with its red and black and gray
floral patterns typical of the period when the building
was built. A short while ago he had climbed these
same stairs, walked on this same carpet. Now he descended the stairs as if nothing had happened. The
same man as before. But under his arm he was carrying the set of X-rays that announced his death or, to
be more exact, dated it with certainty. Unconsciously,
he began to run down the stairs, a fox pursued by
hounds. Might as well take advantage of the time he
had left; in three months he'd have to "take it easy,"
not overdo it, be reduced to taking the elevator up
and down, the way the sick and elderly were forced
to do.

When he came to the second-story landing, he sat
down on the top step. He gazed at his hand, at the
pulsating veins, the muscles and tendons. . . . A pale
light filtered through the round windows of the elevator shaft, typical of the apartment houses constructed
in the 1930s, a light Paul found as lugubrious as the
stingy lights in the stairway. Paul turned his hand over
and looked suspiciously at his lifeline: it was considerably longer than the hamster's predictions. So the
lifeline had lied. He took a cigarette out of his pocket,
hesitated a moment before lighting it, then took a
long and deliberate drag. Not that he was trying to

defy fate or challenge the quacks, but he felt his throat constricting, felt something invading his eyes and nose, deforming his mouth. He had not cried in eight years, not since his mother's funeral, in fact. And as he burst into tears for the first time in eight years, he had a fleeting, furtive moment of shame at the thought that the tears he was shedding were for himself.

II

IT WAS THE END OF SEPTEMBER. The weather in Paris was lovely, a kind of Indian summer, with a light wind, accompanied by occasional gusts, that was still pleasantly warm. A wind that toyed with the clouds above, transforming a dark, narrow street into one drenched in bright sunlight, then back again, with disconcerting speed. Paris, Paul thought, was a zebra, a series of black and white stripes.

Standing on the threshold of the porte cochère, Paul gazed out at the city — his city — which was caught in the thrall of autumn, and for the first time in his life he was irritated by its charm. His car was parked only a stone's throw away, and he dashed toward it with his head lowered, as if the passersby could somehow have detected, beyond the sport coat and the thick lock of bobbing hair, the face of a man condemned to death. The indecent, embarrassing, pitiful face of a man only half alive. He had to rid himself of this shame, this brand-new feeling of guilt that was suffocating him, that was affecting him to such a degree that it took him a good ten seconds to get his car key into the ignition. He started the car, then gunned the motor and sped off with a screech of tires on pavement; the car, unused to such rough treatment, roared, coughed, and stalled. Paul laid his head back against the headrest and closed his eyes. More than anything else, he had to rid himself of this nausea. This impression of emptiness, of internal fragility, the idea that his bones could — no, would — crumble beneath the weight of his body, crumble and turn to dust, this about-face of both mind and body (in sync, for once, through a combination of panic and nostalgia) was unbearable. How much he already missed his beloved Paris! . . . not, though, without a nagging feeling of spite, as if someone had taken it from him. . . . But who? Paul had long ago ceased to believe in God, and in fact had no regrets about his loss of faith — except when he ran into real trouble, as he had today. No, it was not a god — Catholic or Protestant or whatever — nor was it fate or anything or anyone else that had suddenly stripped him of all his worldly goods and possessions. Paul had never believed in anything beyond the natural affinity between himself and his existence. He was a happy-go-lucky, naturally positive person, and his innate cheerfulness, like his fits of anger and the way he related to other people, was contagious. Yes, he had been blessed with more brains and ability than most of his friends, but today all those talents and gifts had fallen away, leaving him alone, naked, and ill in the eyes of the rest of the world. But — and he was sure of this — those who had loved him or looked up to him till now, some for as long as thirty years — whether they were his friends, his lovers, or merely some passing fancy —

every one of those who had willingly, and gratefully, followed in the wake of his vitality and energy would, as soon as they knew he was sick, start avoiding him, as if he had been misleading them all these years. They would feel sorry for him, of course, but they would also shy away from him. And at this point how could he change everything, think of his life as anything other than the long, continuous gift it had always been? Of course, the feeling, the sensation of life — of his life — had never left him for very long, but he had never known, never been able to figure out, what "to live" and "to expect from life" really meant in their magnificent, precarious fragility. No one had ever been able to understand that. And no one ever would.

He drove along the quais of the Seine, free of tourists now that autumn was here, past the Portes d'Asnières and Gennevilliers. There were a number of dilapidated barges, several half-sunken boats, a smattering of makeshift huts; the islands in the Seine in this part of Paris were a real shambles, half abandoned, a wasteland fast becoming a real slum. He saw some fishermen lackadaisically holding their lines; some people, warmed by the September sun, were lolling on the new-mown grass reading their newspapers. Somewhat to his surprise he did not envy them, and yet he knew that next fall they would still be there, they would see the leaves turn orange and red, and he would not. But that was a notion he found impossible to comprehend. And if his own inner motor was sputtering, that of his car was still going strong. It was a powerful motor that purred reassuringly, and when he had bought the car not long before, the salesman had told him with a laugh that the motor was so good it would probably outlast him. Funny he should remember that. They had both had a good laugh, amused and incredulous at the thought, the way we often laugh at something without thinking. Now the remark seemed more like a prediction than a joke.

It was past noon, and Robert would have gone out for lunch if he didn't get a move on. Robert would tell him what to do. He was a man, a friend. Someone who was surely going to help him one way or another. Unlike Helen, who found Robert egotistical, or Sonia, who simply found him vulgar, Paul thought of Robert Gaubert not just as his best friend but as his only friend. It was not in Paul's makeup to dwell overly on his relationships with men, but in the case of Robert, yes. He knew he could count on Robert for strength and support.

Gaubert's offices overlooked the Seine, just this side of the Port de Paris. Paul and Robert never went to see each other in their respective offices, and Paul's arrival seemed to upset Robert more than it pleased him.

"He's been on the phone all morning," his secretary murmured. "London, New York, Hamburg . . ." Her tone seemed a mixture of pride and concern, as if she felt personally responsible for the phone company's technical prowess that enabled her boss to call all over the world, but at the same time worried that she would somehow be held accountable for the considerable bills he was running up as well.

When he entered Robert's office, Robert motioned for him to have a seat. Robert and Paul could have passed for brothers, or perhaps cousins: similar builds, the same way of carrying themselves. But Robert was less muscular, less athletic, and he had less success with women than Paul did. Paul's jokes about Robert-the-womanizer had never struck Robert as very funny. Helen, though she pretended to like him, was malicious and jealous, and a poor judge of her husband's male friends. Gaubert was one of the few she allowed to slip past her guardhouse.

Paul, sitting across the desk from Robert, could not refrain from noting, as he always did each time he came here, how pretentiously modern this office was. A great time to be dwelling on aesthetic details!

"A rare treat! So tell me what brings you here." Robert smiled. "In need of an alibi?"

"No," Paul said. "The fact is, I've just had a lousy bit of news."

"You in love?"

The telephone rang, and Gaubert picked up the receiver. "Excuse me a second. Yes? All right." He put his hand over the mouthpiece and said, "It's London." And with that he started speaking fairly fluent English. The man's made progress, Paul thought. In all sorts of areas . . . Of course, he had learned English using the latest book-and-tape method — Helen had listened to some of the tapes and found them hilarious — but the fact remained that now Robert spoke passable English whereas he, Paul, still stumbled and stammered. This said, he was glad he hadn't wasted his precious evenings learning English, however helpful it might have been in the long run. Now what good would it have done him? *To be, or not to be: that is the question.* Indeed, that was the question. . . .

Gaubert hung up. "Sorry about that," he said. "I'm in the midst of negotiating an exclusivity with CBS for all of Europe. How about that, Robert? The entire European continent. No small potatoes, eh?"

"Great," Paul said. He gave a deep sigh. "That's really great."

Robert leaned across the desk, in his best businesslike manner. "I have a feeling your heart wasn't in your congratulations," he said. "What's the matter?"

"I went to see a doctor this morning," Paul said. "I have . . . a thing in my lungs. He tells me I have six months, give or take."

Gaubert slumped back into his seat, his face suddenly dead serious, even, Paul thought to himself, marmorean. The face of a stoic Roman hero beset by problems who refuses to show any distress. "Actually," thought Robert, and he found the notion almost funny, "it's *my* distress he's not showing."

"Okay, let's have the details, please. What did they do to you? X-rays? What about a CAT scan? Is your doctor any good? Who is he anyway?"

"He's Dr. Jouffroy's replacement. I've been with Jouffroy for years. This new guy's a total jerk, but he's a good doctor, yes."

The phone rang again and Gaubert picked it up, his face still expressionless. "Sorry, my friend. Will you forgive me again?" he said, but his tone was more imperious than begging. And again he launched into fluent English, glancing sternly from time to time in Paul's direction, before he lost his temper with the party on the other end, turned unpleasant, and hung up without so much as saying good-bye.

"They think they can do anything they goddamn well please, these Americans!" Robert fulminated. "They think they own Europe! . . . But back to you. How can you trust a doctor you don't even know, for Chrissake? A *replacement* doctor! You must be joking. Paul. You're going to outlive us all, of that I'm sure. Want to bet?"

Damn sure bet, that one, Paul thought ironically, but he decided not to dwell on it.

"I had all the fancy tests," Paul said. "CAT scans included. Several, in fact."

He heard a low moan emerge from his lips and hated himself. He was horrified and ashamed.

The phone rang again, and Gaubert swore as he grabbed it. "Can't they leave me in peace for a few goddamn moments?" He closed his eyes in exasperation, then punctuated the remarks on the other end with an occasional comment: "Yes, okay, I prefer that. I said, I prefer that! But at what price? Okay, okay! What? I *am* listening to you! Yes, yes, I'll pick you up at Roissy airport on Friday. What time is your plane coming in? Three-thirty. I'll be there. . . ." He lifted his eyes and stared at the wall above Paul's head, then raised his fist in a sign of victory. "That seems fair enough. Right. Right. See you Friday." And he hung up.

"Really . . . I can't believe these people. If they think they can . . . Oh, sorry, Paul. I'm going to tell them that if this guy calls back I'm not in." He picked up the phone and instructed the receptionist to hold all calls, no matter how urgent. "And that includes the pope," he said, thereby proving no doubt that he was ready to risk excommunication in the name of their friendship.

"Let's get back to what's important. Now listen to me, pal, and listen to me carefully. You're upset — that's not a strong enough word, but you know what I mean — which is only normal. I mean, there's good reason, God knows. But I frankly don't believe you. If a Dr. Barondess or Lingrès or some other top specialist comes up with the same diagnosis, then of course . . . But today you were in the hands of some second-rate quack, I guarantee. . . . Where are you going?"

Paul was on his feet. He wanted to get out of there, for no rhyme or reason. This fancy office was getting more and more on his nerves.

"I have to run," he said.

"Above all, not a word to your family," Gaubert suggested. "Or you'll have to answer to me."

He smiled at Paul, who noted that Robert's face was slightly flushed. As he accompanied Paul to the door, Robert gave him a hearty slap on the back, as if to make sure that the body — and therefore his remarks — was still solid.

"You'll see," he said. "You'll see that I'm right. You're not the sick type. In fact, I've never even seen you slow down, much less call in sick. If you have trouble getting an appointment to see Barondess, give me a call. My sister-in-law and Barondess's wife are like this" — and he joined his thumb and forefinger. Then, contradicting his words of optimism and encouragement, he knocked on the nearest piece of wood. Robert's parting words — "Call me right away! Call me the minute you have the results!" — echoed in Paul's ears as he fled down the hallway, fleeing what exactly he didn't know.

He climbed into his car and drove away. He couldn't fathom Robert's reaction to the news, and found it impossible to understand how or what he felt. Poor Robert: his cancer couldn't have surfaced at a worse time, not only for himself but for Robert as well.

He had apparently left the car radio on the whole time, and he leaned down to turn it off, his reactions too slow apparently, for the blare of the horn seemed to explode inside his head. A truck had just exited the warehouse on his right and turned onto the boulevard. He saw Paul barreling toward him, going too fast, too fast to avoid an accident, he was sure, and the truck driver hit the horn with all his might. Paul jammed on the brakes and swung the steering wheel hard right, which bounced him up onto the sidewalk, then hard left, which took him onto the divider between the two lanes of the boulevard, which, miraculously, was empty; at that point he somehow managed to maneuver the car back onto the roadway. He had come within a hair of having an accident, a serious accident, and in his rearview mirror he could see the truck, which had stopped, and several people looking and pointing in his direction. He hadn't run over anyone. He hadn't killed anyone. And here he was running away, fleeing the scene of the crime. Man, had that been close! His legs were jelly, as they always were after an accident or a near accident, and for a brief moment he congratulated himself on the fact that his reflexes were still intact, when all of a sudden he slammed his fist hard against the steering wheel. Damn! Damn! Damn! What a complete ass he was! He had just been presented, on a silver platter, the gift of a lifetime, the solution to all the endless days and nights of agony and suffering that lay ahead. He hadn't sought it, he hadn't asked for it, but there it had been offered him. But no, he had to be smart, he had to be clever, he had to call on his good old reflexes to avoid the inevitable accident, the only thing that could have saved him from hurting those he cared about: a clean, quick, unintentional death. And with his legs still shaking, his mind in a state of absolute fury, he stepped on the gas and roared away, as if another miracle might lie just down the road, another chance to die a swift and flaming death might once more be offered him on a silver platter.

He was still furious with himself as he crossed the Saint-Cloud bridge, nor did his anger subside during the several minutes it took him to drive through the park. There wasn't another car in sight, and he noted that here the leaves had not yet begun to turn. He pulled over and stopped, turned off the ignition, stepped out of the car, and leaned against the door on the driver's side, feeling the warm metal press into his back. He took a deep breath, stretched, and gazed around at the peaceful setting — without deriving one iota of satisfaction from its beauty. Ah, there was the rub. For several weeks no doubt he would be able to go about his life normally — even happily — but there would always come a moment when some detail would be lacking, something would be askew, and the whole house of cards would come tumbling down. He left the car and walked through the park for a good five minutes, then lay down on the grass beneath a tree. It was strictly forbidden to walk on the grass, much less lie down on it, but there was no cop — in fact, no other human being — anywhere in sight. His head was nestled against the tree trunk, his legs stretched out in front of him. He watched the playful movement of the leaves at the top of the tree, way up there, and tried to figure out whether it was a chestnut, a beech, or an elm. And he realized that he really couldn't tell one tree from another. The elms, he knew, were dying in droves this year, the victims here as in other countries around the world of Dutch elm disease. It was like their cancer. This year's statistics would show that so many people had died of cancer, and so many elm trees had yielded to the dread disease. He, Paul, like this tree above (if indeed it was an elm) would be classified as a victim of this year's — or maybe next year's — death toll.

And men, like the elm trees, struck down in the fall,
Grew thinner and thinner and did not attend the
ball. . . .

He enjoyed making up nonsense verses, doggerel. Now there was a word he loved: "doggerel." Doggerel verses had the same ability to move him that certain songs on the radio did, conjuring up some unexpected memory. He had more or less classified his memories into three distinct categories: those that moved him or affected him deeply; those that amused him; and those that left him feeling guilty or made him want to run away. He thought he had tagged them all. Where, then, did the memory that now flooded his mind emanate from? A memory of morning, an open window overlooking the village square, he and his grandmother in the window, she holding his hand, and his boyish voice asking the village orchestra to play over and over again the same tune, filled with flourishes and drumrolls, which delighted him. And the other memory of a little red-faced boy who recited poems — doggerel verses, according to his father? And he, Paul — before he had wanted to grow up and become a fireman, an electrician, a jet pilot, an actor — had aspired to be a poet, a troubadour who would go from town to town and village to village reciting verses. "My little troubadour," his grandmother used to call him as she hugged him, during those long winter days when his parents had packed him off to stay with her in her huge old house. Five years later he had been ashamed of her, and of himself. And when he was fifteen he had been ashamed of his parents. How brief our lives are, he thought, how fragile little old ladies, and how ungrateful little boys.

He no longer saw the shimmering green leaves above him as so many separate entities but as one blurred green mass. One continuous, uninterrupted wave of warm, green water that he let flow gently over his cheeks in this deserted park. Probably the tears of the troubadour.

III

IT WAS ONE OF THOSE CLASSIC, old-time Paris cafés that doubled as tobacco shops. They had fallen out of fashion, and were few and far between these days, but Paul always enjoyed them. Their clientele was inevitably a mixture of regulars who lived in the neighborhood, plus a smattering of people who were either out of work or had nothing better to do with their time than sit in a café staring out the window. The owner, standing behind his zinc bar, flanked by his cash register on one side and the tall ranks of cigarettes on the other, looked for all the world like a tyrant surveying his kingdom, as jealous as a Jesuit monk, and he looked at Paul, the newcomer, with a large measure of suspicion and distrust, which for a moment almost threw Paul off balance. Paul nonetheless approached the bar, leaned on it, ordered a glass of white wine, and in a moment of spontaneity, ordered "drinks all around." Paul hadn't set foot, much less spent time, in a café like this for a long time. And a whole world, a whole atmosphere, made up of an uneven mixture of drinks, of friends and acquaintances, of penny-arcade games, of arguments, of silly bets made after the third or fourth drink, bets that would never be remembered and never paid off, came flooding back to him, as a real-life fairy tale: unreal, unreal and pleasant.

"So what about that round on me?" Paul repeated, leaning on the counter directly opposite the owner, who was still eyeing him suspiciously.

It should be noted that the times when a customer would offer drinks all around had long since passed. One did not offer free drinks to one's fellow man anymore without some compelling reason. The time of "freebies" was dead and gone. The internal revenue had seen to that: gifts could not be accepted or tolerated, and certainly not written off (a subject that had given rise to a heated conversation during a recent dinner party). Paul remembered theorizing nostalgically about how much better off turn-of-the-century gentlemen had been than we are today. They may have been taken for everything they had by the courtesans of the era, but at least they had derived some pleasure from their ruin, and it was not accompanied by the barbarity that marked the tax department's methods of money stripping. Which reminded him: what was he going to leave his wife? Or rather: his women. The recent recession had hurt him badly, and at this point he owned only one-third of his architectural firm, which, to put it mildly, was struggling. And the Poissy project, which was so near and dear to him, where aesthetics and ethics had finally come together in a single, major work, this project of which he had so rightly been proud and for which he had fought for two years, now seemed, he was amazed to discover, empty and unimportant. In the space of one brief hour he had distanced himself from a project that had long been the focal point of his professional life, a project that, only yesterday, had excited him and fired his imagination. But what, he thought, could withstand the knowledge that death lay just around the corner? Not only what, but who? A great love, perhaps? . . . Which left him out: he had no great love in his life. And never would.

The owner, meanwhile, had played his role and poured drinks for everyone in the café. Glasses were raised to Paul, and he could see, behind the raised glasses, inquiring looks, as if the customers wanted to know what it was they were celebrating. And once again a wave of shame washed over Paul, a feeling of embarrassment that he was not like everybody else, that he had become a man without a future, a man without any plans or projects, a man henceforth stripped of all desire. How many fellow creatures had he passed unknowingly in the night, people who, like himself, had been deprived of all their inner resources, and at the same time felt ashamed? No, it was safe to say that there was nothing romantic about not having a future. The charm of living, of life itself, was built on the notion of time with a capital T, time in the Proustian sense of the term. Proust! Now there was another rub: he had vowed to read, or reread, all of Proust before he died. Now he would not have the time, assuming of course he still had the desire. As if he could still desire anything . . . Unless he could bring himself to tell someone the awful truth; share the bread of sorrow with those who cared about him the way he had always shared with them the bread of plenty. And there were legions with whom he had shared his bounties. Then he thought of those he had neglected, dropped, forgotten. He had been loved for his good health, his high spirits, his equilibrium, his zest for life, his curiosity, his forgiving nature. What would be left of all those qualities three months from now? Nothing.

He looked at the clock above the bar: one o'clock. He had arrived at the hamster's at eleven. And he had been there for about an hour. Only an hour. Or: what an endless hour? You could look at it either way, and apply either criterion to the longest, the most serious, the most insignificant, hours of the rest of his life. He motioned to the owner in the direction of his store of white wine, and at the same time he took a banknote from his pocket and slapped it on the counter.

"Another round. One more round for everybody," cried the owner and the waiter in unison, who now realized that they had a live one here, an authentic big-time spender in their midst. Once again glasses were raised to Paul, and toasts offered: "Thanks." "To your good health." "Appreciate it." "Another glass of white wine over here." "Here's looking." The fact was, Paul was not only good-looking, there was something engaging and easygoing about him. Plus a certain rugged quality that made men, as well as women, like him instinctively. (Women tended to detect something troubled beneath the outwardly peaceful surface, however.) But for the moment he was the anonymous newcomer at the Zinc du Port, as his new haven was called.

"And what are we drinking to?" inquired Paul's neighbor, who had had the foresight to empty his glass before asking, to avoid having to toast a nutcase or a cuckold, if it turned out Paul was either. Or worse. This way — having downed his wine — his honor was intact.

"Let's say . . . to your good health," Paul responded. "To mine. To the good health of everyone. To life!"

"Here, here!" chorused the barflies and regulars. "Here, here!" And with the ice now broken, several clients felt it their obligation to thank this unknown patron of the bottle and offer a round in turn. The owner, grateful to this generous stranger for having single-handedly doubled his afternoon business, began looking at him with greater and greater affection as one bottle after another was emptied.

The café was a clean, well-lighted place, and when all was said and done this wonderfully pleasant white wine, which little by little was replacing the blood in Paul's veins, was pretty treacherous. It had become impossible for any gentleman worthy of the name to refuse a proffered glass of wine; and if some customers did not feel obliged to pay a whole round, they nonetheless felt it their bounden duty to offer a glass to the "newcomer."

It was one-thirty, two o'clock. They had all apparently forgotten the sacred ritual of lunch. Paul's fellow barflies were turning out to be really nice guys, aside from one obsessive type who couldn't stop telling him — for the third time, as Paul recalled — about the top five winners among his wife's many lovers, a story that of course fell apart in the end. Then there was another guy who claimed he worked for the secret police and knew every sordid detail of political malfeasance in the corridors of power, which he went on about at great length without offering any specifics. And he would inevitably finish with: "Not a word, okay? Just between the two of us. Word of honor, right? From my lips to God's ear . . . Believe me: my lips are sealed!" and he would punctuate his bellowed secrets by bringing his forefinger and his glass — which seemed at this point to be working at cross-purposes — simultaneously, and ever more frantically, to his mouth.

Without trying to keep up with the guzzlers, Paul was downing one glass after the other and chain-smoking as well. And the more alcohol he absorbed into his system — he was an appreciative social drinker, but not an alcoholic by any means — the more he went about setting his life in order. An hour before he had been an unwelcome stranger in this café, into which he had walked at random, and now he felt increasingly that he was a welcome guest (albeit a guest all the more appreciated in that he was paying for most of the rounds). He was the friend, the neighbor, the equal of all these guys, who also were beginning to think of him as their friend, their neighbor, their equal. Sickness and death retreated before him, offering a thousand excuses as they departed: true, he was going to die, but the more he thought about it the more he reminded himself that it was the hamster's word against his. True, he perhaps had only six months to live, but he was determined to live them like a real prince. He'd go head to head with these germs or microbes or whatever they were; he had, thank God, both the character and courage to face them without flinching. He would die, but death implied moving to another life, going to another planet, for something within him — his soul perhaps? — was immortal. Not in the grandiose, or even Catholic, sense of the term, but in the positive, upbeat, living acceptation.

His red blood was probably too red, even if it was, as Helen claimed, from a long line of blue bloods — Helen had recently and secretly become enamored of the aristocracy. His blood, which, now that he thought of it, had probably turned into the French flag — blue, white, and red — with the addition of all this white wine . . . where was he? ah, yes, this blood would stand him in good stead for a good long time. How about all those cases he had heard about, incomprehensible and little understood — especially by the doctors and specialists, to be sure — where people had been given only a short time to live and had defied all the predictions by living for another twenty or thirty years? Why shouldn't he be in that category? It was just as crazy to think that he would die as it was to believe he'd survive, when all was said and done. Or else he would go to Lourdes and pray for a miracle, yes, he'd go with Helen on one arm and Sonia on the other — which would be a miracle in itself — and both the women would pray for his recovery at the same time they were praying for their rival to be struck down on the spot. He pictured their three silhouettes in front of the grotto, which in his mind's eye looked more like the grotto of Louis II of Bavaria than the grotto at Lourdes, but that was because he had seen the Visconti film and had never been to Lourdes. Paul burst out laughing at the thought, but the laugh was ill-timed because it came just as the man next to him was describing what had gone wrong between his wife and her third lover, and the man was so vexed he got up and stalked away. The man from the secret police took advantage of the situation to slip onto the empty barstool next to Paul.

"Tell me, pal, what exactly *are* we celebrating? I mean, no kidding. I won't tell a soul, I promise, you can count on my utter, I mean *utter,* discretion. My lips are sealed! But I would like to know. Must be something special. Your mother-in-law just die?" And he roared with laughter at his own joke.

"No, can't say she has," Paul said. "At least not yet. But that's not a bad idea. Not a bad idea at all," he went on, for the fact was Paul detested his mother-in-law.

It made such good sense! He hated his mother-in-law, and he cheated on his wife with a younger mistress: he was truly the prototype of the mediocre Frenchman. The only difference between him and his peers was that he was destined to die earlier than most; and besides, what made it different was that he was aware of it. So on with the celebration! Celebrate without saying what or why you're celebrating.

That's the way it was. It was absurd, but nobody should be under the mistaken impression that he was going to spend his last months trying to figure out

"why." Like most of his friends and acquaintances, he
spent his life — and had done so since he had been
old enough to earn his own living — answering questions that began with "what." The "whys" and
"wherefores" would have to remain the province of
adolescents and philosophers. There was nothing to
indicate they should become the province of the
dying — or, more accurately, the future dead. For
Paul felt more alive than he had ever felt, thanks no
doubt to the white wine he had drunk, to the alcohol
that had in this century been the object of so many
unjust attacks; alcohol, which was the friend of man,
the panacea of his soul, his body's faithful accomplice.
How could one not recognize its countless virtues?
The immediate, therapeutic effect; the powerful, positive, efficient results it produced? How could one
denigrate alcohol-the-benevolent, the wondrous gift
of the gods that had the rare ability to lift life's bur-
dens from one's weary shoulders, to gladden the heart
of the poor and downtrodden, render dullness poetic,
give courage to the meek and the timid? Not to mention its ability to introduce immoderation into the
world of general mediocrity. How can we not fail to
give thanks to this admirable crutch, which has the
capacity to bring comfort to whatever in the human
spirit is lame or crippled? Why don't we spend more
time and effort examining the relationship between
alcohol and intelligence, the origin of and profound
affinity between the two? Now Paul was able to think
about his foreshortened life, and the importance of his
death, with resignation, lucidity, and equanimity, as
peacefully at this moment as an hour earlier it had

horrified and panicked him. Now Paul could contemplate calmly the possibility that he could take care of the problem himself, in six months or in two days if he wanted to, since he had at his disposal his trusty hunting rifle. Two hours before, that idea had struck him as terrifying, melodramatic, impossible; now the solution seemed to him both relevant and convenient. He had entered this bar a lamb; he was leaving it, thanks to the wine, a lion.

He had every intention of coming back to the Zinc du Port, and if he returned on a Sunday he would surely be invited to lunch, together with a few other privileged regulars, to share the specialty of the house, cooked up by the owner's wife: stuffed cabbage. The café owner really liked him, Paul could tell, and it wasn't just superficial. So did the other customers. And he swore by all that was holy that he would indeed come back. If in six months he hadn't managed to find a free Sunday to join these fine people for lunch, then he simply wasn't worthy of living any longer. And that was a fact.

IV

THE SUN HAD FINALLY WON the battle of the weather, its enemy, the lowering clouds, having beaten a hasty retreat across the sky, and Paul was about to congratulate the sun on its victory when he thought, No, congratulations were not in order; it was the wind that had done it. In the weather war, what a difference between the bright sun, which one took for granted, and the rain, which displayed its black squadrons, paraded its scudding clouds, to mark its victories.

Lunchtime was over, and he couldn't remember whether he had made an appointment with someone or other. If so, he had stood the person up. He drove aimlessly up and down the streets, then pulled up and stopped in front of the Left Bank Air Terminal, the Invalides. The Alexander III bridge, its freshly gilded ornamentation sparkling in the slanting autumn sun, lay directly ahead of him. It was on a day like this — in fact at this very spot — that he had met Mathilde — that is, met love, for she had loved him as deeply as he had loved her. But for her, love had lasted only a year.

Mathilde, whom he had forbidden himself to think about for so many years now. Mathilde . . . Was he going to die without having seen her again? Probably just one more of those inconceivable, incomprehensible things of life. After all, the notion of dying without having seen Mathilde again was no more absurd than the idea of living without her had been at a certain point in his life. . . . One thing he was sure of in any case was that during the brief time he had left he had to turn his back on the past. He could in no wise wallow in what his life had been up till now, for the simple reason that it was someone else's life. Another man, a man who had never even thought about death, much less assigned a specific date to the dread event. He must learn to live without a past — for that past would be inexact, untrue — as he had to learn to live without a future, since he had none. He must learn to live in the present. Easier said than done! And yet, irony of ironies, how often had he boasted in his other life — his life before today — that he lived only in and for the present. And how often had others reproached him for that carpe diem attitude. For him, it fitted what he considered his epicurean character, his lust for life, his tendency to do his own thing come what may — all of which gave comfort to his pride and pleasure. But on the threshold of what lay ahead of him, there was no longer any word or theory that could justify pleasure for pleasure's sake. The terms "sensuality," "paganism," "present," "pleasure," and "happiness" made as little sense as did "masochism," "perversion," "heroism," "narcissism" — dry, meaningless words used to explain or justify the various and often contradictory behavior that constituted any person's life, changes that could just as easily stem from overeating at lunch as they could result from unrequited love. There was nothing, absolutely nothing he was sure of any longer. Yes: he was certain of having been miserable or happy; he was sure of having done his best to control his feelings in one way or another. He was sure of having been ambitious when he was twenty, of having dreamed of building palaces and stately structures — dreams that very quickly had to be modified, scaled down to solidly constructed houses, in which the bathrooms didn't fall apart the first time there was a flood and the roof didn't leak the first time it was hit by a strong wind. That was the basic task of any architect worthy of the name, wasn't it? No easy task, either, especially if you were a government employee or had to answer to the state.

The more he thought, the more confused he became. He only wished he could have talked to a real friend, someone like Michael, who had known him for years. Michael, who had been his closest friend in college, then at engineering school, with its classrooms blue with cigarette smoke; and later, during the years they studied architecture together. Michael, whom he had known since they both were teenagers, Michael with whom he had shared girls and the wonders of Paris for four years — or was it five? — shared in the way you do when you're twenty: the world is your oyster, and life is a song — dramatic, immoderate, comical. They had spent whole nights roaming the length and breadth of Paris together, reciting poetry at the top of their lungs — Apollinaire, Eluard, René Char, Baudelaire — to any and all who would hear, or to no one but the wind. Along the quais of the Seine, in crowded nightclubs, standing on park benches. They had wandered and they had rambled, and — sometimes mournfully, sometimes cynically — they had made love with girls who found their antics "adorable." Michael would not have failed him, would not have pretended that he didn't understand or couldn't really believe what Paul was telling him. And Michael would certainly not have kept him waiting while he took phone call after phone call, would not have thought his ridiculous little business affairs were more important than Paul.

But then, how could he be so sure? How did he know what had become of Michael? Maybe Michael had turned into one of these lean and driven men entirely focused on material success. Or maybe Michael had, on the contrary, become a fat slob, done in by life. On the most basic level, a careerist or a failure by society's standards. Or perhaps Michael had evolved into one of those myopic, uncaring men who somehow can't transcend their own concerns, who have no time or inclination for altruism. And for the first time in the two hours since he had left Robert's office, Paul was suddenly filled with a feeling of utter disdain for the man. He had never been a good judge of human nature, according to Helen, who found him morally lax, whereas he, Paul, knew that the problem was simply that he had a hard time making up his mind about people. Slow to judge, and even slower to misjudge. No, Michael would still be the same as ever: Paul would have talked to him about life, about death in general, and about his death specifically; he would have viewed death as a normal, albeit fascinating and lyrical journey, with all its vicissitudes. He would have used that banal illness as a springboard, a basis for thought and reflection, for discussion between them, not — as Robert had — as something incongruous, which he found repugnant, or, worse, refused to accept.

So these next six months were going to be not only cruel but boring. In any case for the new Paul, the ironic and lucid Paul who had emerged out of the blue this morning when the bad news had hit him. A lighthearted Paul who would irritate Paul the sick and suffering, Paul the wounded, Paul the heroic, Paul the sorrowful. A Paul who would necessarily be narrowminded, who would let the world know he was ill, then be ashamed at his admission. A second-rate architect, who was generally liked and who had lung cancer, a womanizer and a liar, a man who was in turn tolerant and cowardly, sentimental and egotistical. Who after all would he have wanted to be? Picasso? Talleyrand? Someone of extraordinary talent and power? Not really; all he wanted to be was himself, which struck him as the ultimate pretension. But all he knew for sure was that if Mathilde had still loved him he would have been a better, happier man — and therefore probably more talented and successful.

Would he have grown tired of Mathilde? Probably not. Every moment of their relationship struck him then, as it struck him now, as a bright burst of fun, or of pleasure; in any case, a moment truly shared. No, he would never have grown tired of either Mathilde's intelligence or her character (which were in perfect harmony), nor would he ever have wearied of the wonderful touch of wildness that was hers. The more he thought, the more he was convinced he would have loved her forever. And what impressed him most was not that, after all this time, he was so sure of his feelings for Mathilde but that he both could and wanted to believe them. Especially in light of the fact that, after their breakup, in self-defense and out of a desire for happiness, an innate need for love, and a refusal to wallow nostalgically in the past, he had systematically refused to see her again, to think about her, even to dream about her. This morning's news that he was going to die had made him turn back to her, made him envision their being together again. . . .

Held up at an interminable red light, he was telling himself all this with such conviction and emotion that the driver in the car next to him was staring over in disbelief. Turning his head as if he were talking to an invisible passenger in the back seat, Paul stepped on the gas, his mood black again. When was he going to stop acting like a normal man, a man of regular habits, an adult? He had to stop pretending he was still leading a normal life. . . . All of a sudden he noticed he was approaching his neighborhood gas station, and pulled in. He told the attendant — a man he had known for five years now — to fill the tank. He gave the man an overly generous tip, which prompted an overly generous smile and "Thank you *very* much."

"Beautiful day, eh?" the attendant said, he for

whom a fat tip always served to chase the clouds away.

"You're right," Paul said. "It is a beautiful day all right. The only problem is, in six months I won't be around to enjoy it. I just got the bad news this morning."

"Come on, you can't be serious." The attendant was smiling just as broadly as before, maybe even more broadly. His customers must have included a fair share of big-time jokers.

"It's no joke," Paul said. "Lung cancer," and he tried looking the attendant straight in the eyes.

"If that's true," the attendant said, "you gotta be *very* careful. Take it real easy. I should know. My sister had a thing with her lungs, and I can tell you it was a big deal. . . . So long. Gotta another car waiting. . . ."

And with that the Attendant in Charge of Pumping Gas moved imperiously toward his next customer, smiling still but only halfheartedly as, with the majestic gesture of someone sowing grain, he was directing Paul and his lungs back into the thick of traffic.

For all the guy cared, Paul could have driven headlong into a brick wall. No skin off the attendant's nose. Paul's tires burned rubber as he hit the accelerator. He was less angry at the attendant than he was at himself. What had he expected? That this Pumper of Gas was going to turn immediately into a Shedder of Tears? That he was going to inundate his overalls with salty sobs? Besides, Paul was not all that faithful a customer anyway, and here he was making a special effort to befriend the guy at the gas station. The guy probably wouldn't even miss his biweekly visits. In fact, when he thought about it, which of the several shopkeepers he dealt with, the people from whom he bought his goods and services, would miss him? He lived a little like a nomad. He bought clothes when and where the urge hit him. When he ate out, there were a dozen or so restaurants he went to more or less at random. He bought his cigarettes at the nearest tobacco shop whenever he ran out. And his food and wine were ordered through his office. No, he couldn't even claim to be anyone's good customer!

Well past two o'clock. What was he going to do with himself for the rest of the day? Sonia wasn't home, he knew. Neither was Helen. He should have gone back to the office and talked with his colleague Jean-Claude, his trusty number two, a man as decent as he was tactful. But he knew the man had his own problems. Besides, hadn't he sworn to keep the news a secret, at least in the office? No, he was alone. He was alone, he was famished, and he was going to offer himself a fantastic, gastronomic lunch. He was not by nature a gourmet, but for once he would force himself to be. Before he died he had to discover and savor all the pleasures he had till now neglected: fine dining, for example. He ran down the list of three- and four-star restaurants he knew, but decided to settle for a place in Montparnasse he liked and where he was known. Besides, since most of the top restaurants in Paris stopped serving at two, he knew it was wisest to opt for the known, where he might have a less than perfect meal but where the maître d' would be sure to welcome him. Now there was one who might be sad to lose him. . . . André, the chef of the Globe restaurant . . . My God, Paul: to what depths have you sunk! Searching high and low, from one end of Paris to the other, for someone who will truly miss you!

Paul felt humiliated and guilty, two feelings he disliked the most.

He felt like doing something ridiculous, and try as he might he couldn't shake the idea. He went downstairs to the rest rooms and telephone. The stairway, of dark tile, was moist and slippery and, like those of all Paris bistros, was poorly lighted. He thought of all the countless times he had descended this staircase, or dozens like it, a song in his heart if not on his lips. How many times had he gone down to call someone he loved, someone he worked with, or someone with whom he simply felt like having a good time? How many times . . . Oh, for God's sake, he had to stop trying to transform his life, or the memories of his life, into a long, boring, repetitive balance sheet.

He went into the men's room, the outer door to which could not be locked. He didn't want to be disturbed, so he took the chair that was sitting in a corner and pushed it against the door handle. He quickly stripped to the waist, draping his suit coat, shirt, tie, and undershirt over the chair. When someone knocked on the outer door, first timidly then more and more insistently, Paul shouted, "Someone's in here!" in a voice loud and authoritative enough, he hoped, to frighten the man away.

Above the sink there was a large mirror lit by a long neon bulb, and Paul looked at himself. A not very attractive, slightly greenish face stared back. His gaze slipped quickly down from the face to the neck, then came to rest on the torso. He looked long and hard at the image before him. He found himself ugly. He found all men ugly, especially when they were naked. And that went for their sex as well, that silly dangling thing between their legs, which he found perfectly ridiculous. In fact he had never understood how women — some women in any case — practically swooned over that unmanageable, graceless, and unruly part of the male anatomy. His eyes sought out that part of his chest beneath which lay the heart, trying to detect a sign of its steady beat. His gaze stopped at a point just below the first two ribs, where a fine forest of blond hair descended to the belly button: there, beneath that spot in his chest, an animal, a many-armed beast, a pitiless insect, was at this very moment living and growing, was slyly sharpening its claws, smacking its lips. Now, at this very moment, in the darkness of the organs, in the somber and bloody magma of his body, this foul, stubborn, invincible something was in the process of destroying him, of bringing him down, depriving him of the sun and the wind, pleasure and beauty, his future and his past. His past: what did any of his friends, and even his family, know about his past? The only one who had a clue was an aunt in the provinces, whom in any case he disliked. So his past, and his awareness of it, was going to disappear with him. All the various Pauls — the little boy, the pimply adolescent, the wild and crazy young man, Paul the insatiable womanizer, Paul the enthusiastic architect — all these Pauls were going to die. There. Right there. And slowly he moved his forefinger toward the guilty area, where the tumor lay — at least where he thought it lay — and around this strategic point he drew a circle. Yes, now, right there, his finger was passing above the beast, and he wondered if the beast could feel it, wondered if perhaps the beast might be afraid, and he pressed his finger hard against the flesh. Then he hit himself so hard in the same place that it almost took his breath away.

He coughed, he was shaking, he was sweating as if he had just boxed a couple of tough rounds. Slowly, very slowly, he began to put his clothes back on, his mind still deaf to the sound of the loud knocking at the bathroom door, as the frustrated and angry customer vented his increasing rage. And when Paul opened the door and emerged from the toilet he passed the man without even seeing him. He had doused his head with water, and as he headed back up the stairs, still out of breath, he slapped his cheeks with a gesture that was almost mechanical. It was only when he reached his table, where his favorite maître d' was waiting, that he was more or less himself again.

"Are you alone today, Mr. Cazavel?"

"We're always alone," Paul said, smiling. He sat down at a table for four with a certain feeling of satisfaction. The table was next to the window, and the afternoon sun poured through at an angle and spilled onto the white cloth. He was alone, yes, but that was because he had chosen to be. All he would have had to do was call Helen, or call Sonia, as soon as he had left the doctor's office, or even at some later point, and by now he would have been surrounded by tender, loving women vying to see what they could do for him. But no, he had had the stupid idea of stopping off to see his dear old friend Robert . . . and at the thought he could feel his lip curling sarcastically. But look on the bright side of it: he had taken a lovely drive along the Seine, even if it was a part of the river that was uncommonly banal; and a truck had come within a hair of speeding up, or making short shrift of, his future martyrdom. And again he became aware of the self-pity filling his mind and felt horribly ashamed. Considering the situation, perhaps it was a normal reflex, but still he refused to allow it in his case. He was not going to give in. He would fight this horrible thing tooth and nail, with any ruse he could find. What did it matter! He only had six months to live. He wasn't going to waste them spending his every waking hour in a state of abject terror, in the horrified certainty of his imminent disappearance. From this moment on he was going to enjoy life as he always had, even if there might be a diminution of the pleasure; he was going to take full advantage of the gifts and bounty that nature had bestowed on him. In the same way he had adamantly refused to let himself mope over the loss of Mathilde, so now he would outlaw once and for all the fear of death from his emotional repertoire, if only out of pride. He was not going to ruin "life."

The maître d' had poured Paul a glass of muscadet from the bottle he had ordered, a light wine especially pleasant to the palate, and Paul sipped it slowly, his eyes half closed. A woman at a neighboring table looked at him with a mixture of pleasure and desire, the way one looks at a well-fed, satisfied animal, the way one looks at a happy fellow creature.

After a hearty four-course meal, and two after-dinner coffees drunk in the golden rays of the slanting sun, and after exchanging a few pleasantries with André, who could not do enough for him (and who was far too gracious and affable for Paul to lay his heavy burden on him), Paul made up his mind to leave the restaurant. Sonia would not be home for another hour. The fashion house where she worked would let her out late today, only after she had paraded for the last, demanding customers, who would frequently ask her to model a particular dress for them two or three times to help them make up their minds. After having paraded for the rich and famous like a haughty priest-ess, with her majestic bearing and gait, Sonia would come home and act like a little girl, curl up on the sofa and whine in a childlike voice. (Paul had had to put down his foot to avoid sharing her apartment with a collection of stuffed animals.) Well, in six months maybe they would console her for the loss of her Big Bear — her native American nickname for Paul.

Meanwhile, what should he do? Go to the movies? No, there was no way he could relate or empathize with the petty problems of the characters. And if he were to hit a comedy, there'd be little chance he would find the damn thing funny. No, there was no way under the sun that he was going to waste any of his precious time on some unknown film director. Nor was there any question of holing up with a pile of mysteries, much less seeing their film adaptations. As for playing mindless card games to take his mind off reality, forget it! Which left open the other end of the spectrum: was he therefore going to plow his way through Proust, haunt the museums and other cathedrals of culture? And then there was the choice of gambling the rest of his life away in casinos. No, not that either. Which eliminated for him both the high and low ends of the scale. Which left a comfortable, and probably utterly boring, middle ground; these next six months were going to be a real ball! No, what I actually need, he said to himself — that is, after I have told both of the women in my life the whole truth — is to take stock of myself. Self-communion. It had been a long time since he had allowed himself the leisure of introspection, and he had to admit that he was looking forward to it with a certain amount of curious pleasure — curious because of the conditions under which he felt compelled to do it; pleasure because, however modest and fragile, it struck him as somehow comforting. Yes, that was the word, "comforting." He was fairly sure he was not going to fall apart; he felt he was able to judge himself without condescension, as he knew he was fully capable of ferreting out his detours and deviations from the truth. It was as if a sudden truce had been declared between his vulnerable self on the one hand and that mocking echo he could hear directly behind it, as if someone had moved in behind the series of counterfeit Pauls the world knew and made him somehow coherent, endowed him with a real, authentic life. "As if death

had given me back my life," he said out loud, and he
burst out laughing at the melodramatic, ridiculous
paradox. And although he had been talking to himself
and laughing as he threaded his way through the
crowded streets, no one turned around wide-eyed to
stare at him. "At least no one noticed me," he told
himself, and then the thought went through his mind
that perhaps he had already crossed the threshold beyond which he didn't give a damn what people
thought about what he did or said. High time, he said
to himself.

Well, if he could get his act together and find his
true center it was entirely possible that he would at
the same time become a fully aware person, which in
turn would clarify his conduct during the coming
months. Just how was that going to come about?
Under what conditions? Suffering, he knew, was out
of the question. Both the sensitive and tender Paul
and the cynical, womanizing Paul — and he was fully
aware of this split personality, which he not only rec-
ognized but nurtured, since he felt it gave him a certain piquancy — had a very low threshold of pain.
Moreover, it seemed to him that from time to time
these two Pauls, these two clichés, were slightly wa-
tered down by the force of circumstance and replaced
by a silhouette, a one-dimensional cardboard cutout
of Paul, around whom bullets whizzed without ever
hitting him. An idealized Paul, affable and supple, because till now he had been spared the actual slings and
arrows of these battles. Yes, it was as if a replica of
himself had been set up in his place — a replica that

was perhaps more accurate, or truer, than the original and, if and when it was necessary, more essential than the other copies.

But this nimble and discreet character would, he knew, turn into an instant coward when his body began to fail him, and he knew there was a fore-ordained timetable for that. Paul was one of those people who could grit his teeth and bear it when the going got tough and yet at the same time would panic if a wasp landed on his body. *Waiting for Pain* was not a play he could star in. So where did he go from here? And with whom? Who would he choose as helpmate? There was always the option of suicide, of course. But that implied being alone. Could he really pull that off alone?

He remembered that when he was a kid he and two or three of his closest friends had sworn in blood what they would do in case one of them ever contracted any illness that was diagnosed as hopeless. They all took an oath to take care of business if such a fate should ever befall any of them. When he was a teenager, he and the Dambiez children — Delphine and her brother Pierre — had been inseparable. And they had remained close through their adult years. Then Delphine was found to have cancer, and he had seen the terrible, inexorable destruction the disease had wrought on the once-ravishing creature. Her obituary spoke of the "long, cruel illness" she had suffered, and Paul remembered visiting her only a few months before she had died to find her curled up in a ball at the far end of her bed, a tiny, trembling creature weighing no more than sixty-five pounds and —

the result of the chemotherapy — completely bereft of her long, flowing hair. And yet neither he nor her brother had been able to "take care of business" as they had sworn, for all sorts of reasons, starting with the fact that Delphine, even when she was alone with one of them, would go on and on about her future projects for the coming winter. She planned to rent a chalet in the mountains, she had endless business ventures she wanted to pursue. In other words, she was going on with life. A fantasy life, to be sure, and one that alternately broke the heart or gave comfort to her friends and family, who simply couldn't cope with the widening gap between visible reality and her unassailable projects. Delphine's physical suffering had been especially bad during the last four months of her life, and a dozen times Paul had been on the verge of asking her whether their oath was still valid. But each time he had refrained, for he realized that the mere fact of posing the question was tantamount to acknowledging that she was dying, and that she adamantly refused to admit. Or else she didn't want to admit it any longer. When you spend several days in the full knowledge that you're going to die, there comes a point when you can't deal with it anymore. Actually, the window of opportunity to do something about it — to take care of business — is very narrow. Courage and lucidity, it would appear, yield quickly, very quickly, to hope and illusion. To the refusal in any event of that deplorable platitude, that banal carelessness, which would have you dead even before you've had time to cope with the idea.

Which brought him back to his own situation: after

this first naked, unequivocal, and very strange day he was going through, it was not going to be easy facing up to his own death again. Maybe the first signs of pain, of physical suffering, would jolt you into recognizing the downward path you were facing. When that day arrived he would have to make sure he had all his ducks lined up. Then it would be too late to ask a doctor or pharmacist to give him what he needed. Too late to head for a gunshop to buy the necessary weapon. If all systems failed, he told himself again, there was always his hunting rifle. . . . And then he remembered that he had loaned the rifle to his brother-in-law — what a jerk, that guy; all he does is borrow things from me. Anyway, he must make a point of getting it back. He was in luck: it was September, and hunting season had just opened, so he had a built-in excuse.

Then he started imagining the hunting rifle, and the more he thought the more he realized that was not exactly a piece of cake either. You fire the damn thing with your big toe, he remembered reading somewhere. But he was so awkward, even using his hands, that he could picture firing the weapon with his clumsy toes and, instead of hitting himself, totally destroying one of Helen's prize antiques. . . . There was also some other way to do it, where you tied a piece of string to the trigger, wound the string around the open door, and held the other end in your hand. . . . Lord only knows exactly how that might work. Anyway, the idea was to make sure the gun was pointed precisely in the right direction. Funny, but when he thought about killing himself, he could never picture its taking place anywhere but in his wife's apartment. It was his apartment too, of course, but morally it was hers. Exclusively. As a sort of conjugal duty, one more, "the last duty but not the least" as Robert would have put it in his impeccable English. To kill himself at Sonia's would have been the most odious, the most flagrant, infidelity, the final proof of a preference that Sonia would ultimately have happily forgone. (And Helen, too, for both women shared a similar pride in their respective homes.) So Helen had every right to blame him for this final "worse" of the "for better or for worse" vow they had solemnly made. The worst? Was this really the worst? A man who commits suicide in his own home? In any event, he knew for sure that he would not feel comfortable doing it anywhere else. . . . The classic idea of committing suicide in a hotel room seemed to him as terrible — if only because of the final solitude — as it was unacceptably conventional. People who committed suicide in a hotel did so because they were "orphans," because they had nowhere else to go, Paul reflected. He had always planned his crazy escapades with meticulous care, while he had been utterly relaxed and haphazard about serious matters. This one fell no doubt into the madcap category, for even in a case like his, suicide was in a sense a provocation, an aggressive act against society. It was a crime of flight, a challenge, an act of refusal vis-à-vis the rest of the world, a final declaration of independence; and in that sense it was a narcissistic act, therefore ultimately pretentious.

He couldn't have cared less. He would kill himself

if he could pull it off, if he wanted to badly enough, if he could summon the courage to overcome his fear of death or, more precisely, if he was afraid enough of what he was going to have to live through. Tomorrow he would go out and buy some vials of morphine and a pack of needles. But he knew he couldn't stand injections; so, however destructive it might be, he suspected the rifle would win out over the needle.

Now you walk through Paris, all alone,
Among the madding crowd but still alone . . .

Who in the devil was that by? Ah, yes, Apollinaire. From the piece called "Zones" that precedes "The Song of the Man Unloved." Less well known, in fact, but it was the piece he preferred in the whole volume called *Alcohols:*

Close beside you herds of lowing buses lumber by. . . .
The agony of love tightens its grip upon your throat,
As if love will never pass your way again. . . .

Never loved again . . . He would never be loved again. . . . Now, right now, there was this sweet but — let's face it — not very bright young woman who thought she was in love with him. . . . And who therefore did love him; it came to the same thing after all. He loved and hated out of habit; he too was loved and hated by a woman his own age whom he had wronged without wanting to; but also by doing nothing to make sure she didn't suffer. There it was in a nutshell: his emotional life was a useless game, sometimes fun, sometimes not. You can conjure up all the lines you want from Apollinaire, he thought, but it comes down to that. Besides, how many people quote Apollinaire to embellish or conceal the shallowness of their own feelings? At least he had known what it was to be truly in love, and to be loved in return, for a period of several months. That was something. Was it really? Ten months, maybe a year? Yes, it was in fact tremendous if he compared it to the lives of some men he knew. All he had to do was think of the way any number of men his age reacted when they saw an uncommonly beautiful woman. They giggled like schoolboys, exchanged winks of complicity, they fell all over themselves competing to see who would be most smug. Whereas what they should have done once they had laid eyes on that beauty, that inaccessible beauty, is let the blood drain from their faces, let their hearts fill with desire and regret, knowing that beauty would never be theirs. Actually, that was the way Paul reacted. Besides, whether in a museum before a painting that truly moved him or in life, in the presence of a beautiful woman, beauty had never made him laugh or cry or reflect. It always sent him away from its presence filled with desire and repressed anger, with a feeling that stupid fate had conspired to make sure that the painting, or the woman, would never be his.

V

AS MUCH AS, in times gone by, it had seemed absolutely essential to Paul that he be able to pick up the phone and talk to Mathilde, now that he had a pressing reason to do so the urgency had somehow disappeared. She had become a hope among others, a kind of duty owed this sentimental, nostalgic Paul, this sensitive, vulnerable dreamer who presumably was hidden behind the cynical, womanizing Paul, behind this mask and this shield.

Meanwhile, Paul was driving aimlessly through the streets of Paris. In the past ten years Mathilde had moved. She had moved from the rue de Verneuil to the rue de Tournon; she had left the banks of the Seine for the flanks of the Luxembourg Gardens. In short, she had crossed the boulevard Saint-Germain. And in his mind Paul pictured her in her long, fur-collared housecoat, her feet bare in her slippers, her trademark shawl draped casually around her neck, absentmindedly crossing the boulevard Saint-Germain followed by a cohort of lovers — those he knew about, those he did not, and those still to come — all of them bent low as they carried her hundreds of suitcases. And behold! the long line of cars came to a halt on the boulevard like the Red Sea parting for Moses. And to his great surprise he found himself not only driving up the rue de Tournon but, miraculously, finding a parking space in front of a porte cochère, which might well be Mathilde's. He had had no intention of coming here, or parking in this spot, and yet here he was in front of this new porte cochère, completely vulnerable, and he panicked.

What if this was the door to her apartment? What if she came out and saw him sitting here? What in the world would she think? How could he ever pick up the phone then and call her? For he had not planned to contact her till later. After Sonia. After Helen. After his other women, these "next-in-line," these copies of femininity whom he had married, whom he had tried to love and cherish after Mathilde had left him . . . He was turning into a major boor, he told himself. Phony and ruthless. And he was exaggerating everything. He turned the key in the ignition and drove off, heading toward Sonia's. He would park and call her from a pay phone downstairs — for Paul never called on any woman, even if she was the acknowledged mistress, without calling ahead. First out of courtesy, but also because he hated scenes. The role of cuckold was the one he loathed more than any other, and if he was made to play it he preferred not to know about it. "In short," he told himself, "I'm a coward. And a vain coward to boot."

For a long time now Sonia had been working at the fashion house mornings only, except when there was an emergency, and she normally finished up at about one in the afternoon. That timetable enabled Paul to spend what were known at the office as "business lunches" but in reality were three-hour siestas, from which he returned at four o'clock with a smile on his lips and his mind clearly elsewhere. He loved these early-afternoon "thefts," as he called them — thefts from work, from the day's obligations, thefts from the ordinary round of human affairs. That is, he used to love them. For he realized that it had been quite a while since he had sneaked away to Sonia's place; in fact, the idea never even crossed his mind anymore. He simply no longer enjoyed these interludes. And in the light of today's events, the very thought of such an assignation struck him as crude, forced. As much as nights were made for lovers, afternoon assignations, he felt more and more strongly, were the stuff of vaudeville, and he had lost his taste for them. Of course, when he and Sonia went out in the evening he stayed over at her apartment, but his amorous appetite stopped there. Did that mean he was getting old? Or that he loved Sonia less? Both questions, which would have been matters of serious concern the previous day, now seemed trifling. That was the first positive point, the first happy detachment, that he could chalk up to his new situation. He was sure that others would surface in due course.

As he pulled up near her house, Paul asked himself how he was going to break the news to her. There was a florist on the ground floor of her building, whose bouquets had graced Sonia's living room countless times throughout the years, and for a brief moment Paul thought of buying her a big bouquet of chrysanthemums, or better yet of setting up a long-term chrysanthemum account for her at the florist's, so that she wouldn't ruin herself buying flowers for him or his grave. Unfortunately, Paul realized that Sonia would not get the deeper meaning of the floral gift: she would ooh and ah over the chrysanthemums as if he had given her a dozen roses. "Still," he thought, "if she has half a brain she ought to get the message," and he laughed at himself and his own cleverness. And while he was being clever, why didn't he just draw her a little map leading from her apartment to the Saint-Augustin Church, where he would want the funeral services to be held, and from there to the Montparnasse Cemetery, where, if memory served, his family still had a plot? That would be in good taste, with just the proper touch of frivolity thrown in. Paul had never spent much time plowing through the manuals of good manners, but he doubted if any of them contained a chapter entitled "How to Announce to Your Mistress That in Six Months She Will Be Without a Lover — or At Least Without the Current Lover." In any case, tomorrow he would have to make arrangements to take care of her financially; today when he saw her he would reassure her that everything had already been taken care of. Women worry about such things, even if they're very young, and even if they play Back Street to a dozen suitors.

Paul finally settled on a bouquet of two dozen roses, his usual choice, which Sonia adored. He tried to call her three times from a pay phone downstairs, but her line was constantly busy, so he went upstairs and rang her doorbell. She opened the door, and Paul saw a young man seated in an easy chair, dressed in blue jeans and one of those silver-buttoned black leather jackets that Paul detested. They exchanged smiles, as forced as they were ridiculous, and all Paul could think of was that for a moment at least he felt relieved. A few well-aimed barbs aimed at Sonia's infidelity — even if they were not rooted in truth — would make him feel less guilty. For the fact was, however strange it may have seemed, Paul felt guilty about having to tell Sonia the news of his impending death. He was depriving her of one basic element of her life, which she was not only used to but counted on. And for him to play the double role of herald and hero of his sorrow represented for Paul a part beyond his abilities, not to mention that it was inconsistent with his happy-go-lucky attitude.

Sonia was flushed with pleasure — or was it embarrassment? In any case, she simpered, she purred like a cat, it was visible. She had always liked conventional roles. No, not liked — loved, adored. And yet this ambiguous situation — or what could be taken for such — did not seem to bother her in the least. As for the young man, he seemed distracted, almost to the point of boredom, which augured poorly for possible future amorous exploits. What was more, Paul thought, what the young man was wearing was so tight-fitting that it would clearly take him so long to undress — especially to divest himself of his jeans — that he would doubtless have to think twice before indulging in any sport, be it indoors or out.

So Paul sat down in one of Sonia's stuffed chairs, stretched out his legs, and gazed over benevolently at the young man. This rising generation, Paul thought, apparently complains bitterly that the generation immediately above them refuses to yield its places. Well, the members of Generation X — if that's what the new generation was called — ought to lift him onto their shoulders and parade him through the streets, for here he was, just pushing forty, about to pass them his torch.

He heard himself inwardly deploring the complete craziness of today's fashion, and the inconsistencies of the specialized press, and then he was on his feet shaking the young man's hand and saying, nonsensically, "Hope to see you soon." He also saw himself, when Sonia came back into the room, take her in his arms and press her warm, supple body against his, felt her soft hair against his cheek, pulled her right hip and the rest of her body tight against his own hipbone and left leg, pressing against them like the motionless, salacious dancer he sometimes became when he was holding a willing partner in his arms. Sonia laughed. She laughed, and Paul said to himself that before long she wouldn't be laughing anymore, she might even be suffering, and his hope was that she would not suffer all that much. In any event, he would be responsible for the fact that she wouldn't grieve deeply: either because he had not done enough to make her love him profoundly or because he had not been worthy of her love. And if he was hoping that the news that he had only a short time to live would devastate her, it was, he knew, out of pure egotism on his part. And he blamed himself, for if there was one constant in this more or less intelligent comedy that his emotional life had been it was the sure knowledge that he — unlike many men — hated to make a woman suffer, even if she was his own wife.

But would Sonia perhaps blame him one day for not having made her suffer enough? For not having shared the daily ups and downs of cohabitation, not having given her a taste of the "worse" which was part and parcel of the "better" in a real relationship? For Sonia would never have known anything but the "better" (if he could call it the better) of him. What he had given her was only the lighter, the more pleasant side of his present life.

Or would it be Helen whose grief would be greater? Helen, to whom he had indeed given the "worse," Helen who already remembered only that negative aspect of their relationship. Well, Helen was wrong. Actually, he had not given her the "worse" for the simple reason it was not part of his makeup. It just wasn't there. There was "less good," or at most "disagreeable." And besides, they had both enjoyed a good deal of the "better," even if Helen preferred not to remember it now.

Perhaps he should simply say nothing. Lie to them for their sake, not for his. Remain silent. But even as the thought crossed his mind he knew he would never be able to hold out for six months, that sometime down the road he would crack. And besides, one day they would learn the truth, and when they did they would think he had lied to them even about his own death. They would think that he hadn't needed them, that he had not even trusted them enough to let them give comfort to him, even if they hadn't been inclined to offer it on their own. . . . Paul thought of all the people he knew who were vexed or upset when someone failed to ask them a favor — even if it was a favor they would no doubt have refused. No, that would be pointless. In any case, murmured Paul the practical joker, Paul the womanizer, somehow managing to keep his sense of humor, one thing was certain: he would have to tell them both the same day. And he felt with a pang of sadness — or was it self-pity? — that having to repeat the same sad story twice in the same day would make the second telling less intense, less enjoyable. What a waste! But anyway, he would be too overwhelmed with a welter of conflicting emotions (for he knew he was bound to become very emotional) to compare the two versions.

Besides, there was no point in trying to pretend or imagine another alternative; he knew there wasn't any. Since this morning he had known that he was going to die and die soon, and his immediate reaction had been to inform both women in his life so that they could not only take pity on him but help take his mind off his fear. At his age he was not about to change his whole lifestyle, throw everything over and start anew. There was something called "personal code," and something else known as "custom," and he was not about to leave them behind.

It was true that the worst part of this was not that he was going to die in six months but that he was painfully aware of it. And it was true that capital punishment was, for that reason, a frightful, unjustifiable punishment. It was also true that Dr. Hamster was a stupid little jerk.

"What a stupid little jerk," he murmured, and burst out laughing.

"You're talking to yourself now?"

Yes, darling, he is. He was already becoming senile. It was high time to make his exit.

"I have to talk to you," he said all of a sudden.

There, it was out! His duty done. For two years she had shared his life, his life and his bed, with what seemed to be unmitigated joy and pleasure. He couldn't bring himself to sever his ties to her.

"My poor darling," he said.

And suddenly the tears began to flow, and, his eyes closed, he buried his face in Sonia's hair.

"My poor sweet love!"

And he looked at himself, with incredible distress and disbelief, crying for her, for himself. The trusting little boy, the vulnerable and open young man he had been, all these various Pauls, led only to this: this punishment, this pain, this barbarity. What spite! What cruelty! What utter stupidity! All of a sudden he was overcome with an uncontrollable emotion, an emotion that tore him apart, that tore his entire being the way something stuck to the skin has to be torn away. He felt his throat tighten; it was as if he were incapable of seeing or hearing. Something intimately related to him, more intimately than anything he had ever known, was suffering horribly inside him, was writhing convulsively against him. His entire body was in a state of revolt, terrified and deathly ill. It was a lonely pain, explosive and justified, that spread throughout his arms and legs, down to his hands.

The shadows outside were lengthening. And he

acknowledged in that moment of overwhelming emotion, that long and hateful sob, that intimate and unshareable separation of self from self, that he was yielding to the pain. That this pain would never be effaced. Even if he lived to be a hundred. That from this moment forward his life would be forever divided into a "before" and "after." This moment, when for the first time he had faced up to the truth, had acknowledged with a mixture of rage and disgust and hate the strength, the force of his death, acknowledged with impotent fury and total despair that he would be subjected to "that"; this moment when he had opened the floodgates and let in a wave of conflicting emotions he had not known he possessed, emotions he had loathed and till now managed to repress. But suddenly these same emotions had welled up, taken over his being, forced him to recognize not only that they were his but that they would, for the next six months, be his sworn enemy. Suddenly Paul felt as if he were going to be sick; he moaned, "Oh, no," as if he were about to give up the ghost. And he loosened his grip on Sonia, and as if searching for something to support himself, wrapped his arms around his own body.

"Paul, you're not feeling well," said Sonia, shrewd as ever.

It was not posed as a question. She pushed Paul down onto the sofa, then sat down beside him, perched above him, her expression one of complete panic.

"Paul, you're sick. What is it, Paul? Tell me what's the matter, I know you're sick!"

He gazed up at her. He looked at her lovely face, her beautiful eyes, her pretty nose, her ravishing mouth, her gleaming, perfect teeth. He looked at her, saying to himself what a pity it was he was not madly in love with her. Not only a pity but completely unfair. And convenient, too. For how would he otherwise have been able to resign himself to leaving this exquisite face? In his confusion he smiled at her, tried to calm her fears and reassure her, not so much about his state of health as about his feelings toward her.

"Paul, you've got to tell me," she said. "Please tell me what this is all about."

And suddenly she collapsed on his shoulder and began to sob. "I haven't even told what it is and here she is crying on my shoulder," Paul thought — or rather reproached himself. "I must look like death warmed over, and she having not the faintest notion what this is all about." Of course, he was moved by her tears, but he would have preferred that before she had shed them she had dug a little deeper in an effort to find out the truth, or even refused to believe him. But he felt that he had to justify without further ado his own unconditional tears.

"A lousy tumor on one of my lungs," he said.

She took a deep breath, sat up straight, and moved over next to him, her legs curled up under her.

"I should have followed my instinct and left you," she managed after a long moment, her voice shaking. "I bring bad luck. When you look back . . . Two years ago, it was my mother. Then last winter, Anne-Marie . . . And today, you." She shook her head. "I can't . . . I can't bear it. It's just too much."

And with that she burst into tears again. Aside from the unpleasant realization that she had just made him a member of a club he would have studiously avoided, whether he was in the best of health or deathly ill, Paul now saw himself as no more than one of the passive factors of Sonia's grief, not as her only concern. "I can see that I'm going to have to console her," he said to himself, and the thought irritated him no end.

"I swear I never even dreamed of joining the souls of either your mother or your closest friend," he said evenly. The next thing you knew, he was going to have to feel guilty.

"My poor darling," she said, "and here I was feeling sorry for myself. Are you in any pain? Tell me, sweetheart, tell me you're not. . . ."

"No," he said, "I'm in no pain. And they tell me that for three months or so I'll feel as good as ever."

"And of course chemotherapy and radiation and all those things are worthless," she said bitterly, tossing into the garbage in one fell swoop the most recent discoveries of the cancer specialists as well as their hard-fought victories — some ephemeral, some lasting — that filled the pages of the newspapers and the television screens. No, she was ready and willing to admit, without further ado, that his cancer was of the most serious kind, untreatable, deadly. Her intimate knowledge of her lover's taste for extremes must have convinced her on that score.

"You're right," he said, "they tell me there's not much they can do to stop it, or even slow it down. For the moment at least . . ."

"Anyway," she said, "the very idea of seeing you bald, or thin as a rail and all yellow . . . no, I don't think I could have dealt with that." Her voice, he thought, was a shade too shrill as she slumped back into the folds of the sofa. "No, I couldn't imagine you like that," she said, and Paul felt both disturbed and flattered by the thought that, at least aesthetically, Sonia couldn't survive the notion of Paul minus his hair and his healthy complexion.

"I would have taken care of you, you know I would," she sobbed.

He looked at her, slightly embarrassed. Her face was swollen, her eyes brimming, tears were streaming down her cheeks, and her lips were trembling visibly. Not a very pretty sight, actually, when the chips were down. But then who was?

"Are you sure there's nothing they can do?" she asked, but he thought the question was asked more to put an end to the discussion than to seek real solutions, or even crazy ones. Sonia, who was no rocket scientist, had always opted for simple solutions and easy answers.

"How much time did they give you?" she whispered into Paul's ear, very softly, as if it were an obscenity or a secret that some evil god, hidden beneath her sofa, was prepared to redress or unveil.

"Six months," he said, "three of which should be more or less okay." To his surprise, after the extraordinarily violent emotional reaction he had had a few minutes before, he now found himself slightly bored, interested in noting his mistress's reactions more out of curiosity than emotional involvement.

"During these months . . ." she said, and Paul wondered whether she was referring to the three good months or the three that were destined to follow, "we'll be together, won't we? Promise me we'll be together. You'll spend all your time with me, swear you will."

"Of course I will. Of course we'll be together. Besides, I'll have more time to myself now," he said, not sure whether he was telling the truth or lying. He had the feeling that the hardest part was over, and now that they had gotten through that scene, life was going to resume its former course, exactly as it had been before in this well-appointed, sweetly decorated little apartment.

"And will you be able to . . . will you be able to love me the way you used to?" she said, her eyes lowered.

Although reassured — after Dr. Hamster's buxom nurse had done a disappearing act this morning — that his illness was not going to turn Sonia off, Paul could not help equating himself at this juncture — and the analogy struck him as bizarre — to an ear of corn, with so many kernels left that Sonia intended to eat one by one, till there was nothing left but the cob.

Paul felt that they had said all they had to say to each other and didn't know which way to direct the conversation when Sonia blurted out: "But what am I going to do without you?" and she took Paul's neck in both her hands and gazed fixedly into his eyes. But what he saw in her eyes were not the yellowed films of the past but the films of the future: those evenings she spent alone by the fire, those evenings when she went by herself to cocktail parties, those evenings when she came home alone and snuggled down under the covers without a man. . . . And so forth and so on. Improbable evenings, the more he thought about it, considering how pretty she was — and she really was pretty — but the mere thought that that could happen made his foolish heart soften. He acted as if he had not understood her remark and was doing his best to reassure her.

"Don't worry about your future," he said. "I've taken care of everything. I have no intention of leaving you lost and defenseless in this vale of tears, darling. Of that you may be sure."

"Oh, but you're wrong. I'll be completely lost without you," she said, sobbing. "You're leaving me completely defenseless."

So self-interest is not her overriding concern, he said to himself with a kind of grudging recognition. No, she did love him for himself. She may have loved him poorly or well, but she did love him. And she really was going to miss him in her king-size bed, at least for a while. . . . Until such time as decency or desire allowed her to replace Paul with another man, someone as sensual and healthy as he, someone as smitten by her charms as he had been. No, although relatively modest and not overly pretentious, Sonia knew that her body was fully capable of sustaining her for quite a while; in this context, Paul was no longer a strict necessity.

"You're the one who's leaving. I'm the one who's left behind. Who do you think is going to suffer?"

"Don't forget me in the equation."

"You mean physically? I know what physical suffering is. It's nothing compared to grieving. And besides, it's not going to last very long. Three months, isn't that what you said? . . . That's something quite different."

"You're right," Paul said. "But still, it's not what you might call a pleasurable experience. All I ask is that you let me know the moment you don't love me anymore. . . ."

"You didn't have to tell me that!" (Sonia straightened up with an expression admirably close to wounded pride.) "Do you think I'm capable of pretending, my love? I can't believe you said such a thing! Of course I'll never pretend. And what about all our memories? Don't they mean anything to you?"

And the tears began to flow in even greater abundance.

He was disconcerted by Sonia's reactions, and even more upset by the fact that he was enjoying them. She was more egotistical than he had imagined, and less selfish. She was stronger and more optimistic. In short, she was less sentimental than he had thought, but tougher. In a word, she loved only herself. Herself and, for the past two years, Paul, because it suited her purpose to love him. There was no point in making it hard for her. Especially since she would be perfect till the very end. He was crazy, he told himself, his ideas were completely out of control, he was seeing everything as through a glass darkly, nothing was making any sense to him. Actually, he had quickly come to the realization that he was bored with her, but he didn't want to admit it. It was not the time to become bored,

that much he knew. And yet! And yet, since that convulsive moment a little while ago, which he was
deathly afraid might come back to haunt him, since
that crisis and above all since the period immediately
following the crisis — if that was the proper term —
when he had regained control of himself, become
master of his own fate — a cruel master but nonetheless closer to the real Paul than the panic-stricken animal that had possessed him earlier — since that
convulsive lapse of a few minutes ago, he had had
only one wish, and that was to get the hell out of here
as soon as humanly possible. And once outside, he
wanted to take stock and see if that morbid, terrified,
masochistic character had stayed back upstairs with
her, whining and muttering tenderly with her about
the terrible times to come. If the fretful robot he had
become would only be born again in Sonia's bedroom, in her arms . . . In which case he would never
see her again. But perhaps that was no more than one
of the inconsistencies of his short-term future. Perhaps it was one of his silhouettes he had encountered,
one of his unconscious, solitary doubles, as embarrassing as they were embittered, which would emanate from his illness and stalk him relentlessly over
the next few months.

How many profiles would there be of him, how
many imitation Pauls, how many poor copies? How
many wrecks of himself would surface to fight, in a
panic-stricken rage, amongst themselves, squaring off
in the lugubrious, ridiculous ring of his remaining
days to try to sort out the questions of life and death?
Or was it death and life? In his mind he was already

beginning to juxtapose everything in that kind of light. "Good lord, why in the world am I carrying on these endless one-voice dialogues in the first place?" he thought with a tinge of irritation. "I am me, Paul. I'm still alive. In fact, I feel more alive than ever. I'm not interested in this whole story. I can't — and don't intend to try to — make any sense out of it. The only thing I can say about it with certainty is that it's the antithesis of everything I love. The opposite of life, of my life. I even accept the notion of suffering, if I can limit it to certain specific times, but I don't want to suffer randomly, whether it's physical pain or one of these moments of panic or terror that should be the sole preserve of prepubescent girls." And as he finished his train of thought he felt like slapping himself. Still, taking advantage of the fact that Sonia had gone into the bathroom to get a painkiller, he could not repress a moan, and he could feel his face contorted by a combination of embarrassment and rage.

Sonia had gone to get the painkiller not for him but for herself, for the "scene" they had just gone through — like all their scenes — had, despite its extraordinary seriousness, given her a migraine. She was in the bathroom a full ten minutes, presumably looking for the painkiller, and Paul could not help wondering, in a sudden access of anger, how anyone could have a pain in a part of the body that was so seldom used. Paul, who till now had studiously avoided posing that question to her, suddenly felt that he had every right to.

When she finally reappeared, he greeted her, in a learned tone, with: "You have to admit that your migraine cannot be the result of excessive use of your cerebral tissues."

His voice was so low-key and authoritative that for a second Sonia completely missed the anger and irony. Besides, it seemed to her that the situation was far too serious for irony — even from Paul.

"You mean that I don't make sufficient use of my brainpower, is that what you're implying?" Sonia ventured.

"Not at all! Let's merely say that you recognize your intellectual limitations and you don't very often force yourself to exceed them," he reassured her. "The same goes for me, in fact. No point pushing your cranium to speeds beyond its capacity."

"In other words, I'm stupid and happy in my stupidity, is that it?"

"No, darling," Paul protested, his eyes bulging. "That's not what I meant at all! You've got it all wrong. My darling" — forgotten the hamster, forgotten his ex-friend Robert, forgotten too the Zinc du Port and its dubious crew; his penchant for jokes, and the generous amount of white wine in his veins, had done away with all inhibitions — "my dear sweet darling. I meant just the opposite. What I mean is that you use the brains you were blessed with remarkably well, without — thank God — wasting your time on abstractions, which is all to your credit, because people who do are, purely and simply, pretentious asses."

Sonia's face softened, but a tinge of suspicion lingered in her eyes. She was standing in front of Paul, watching her pills dissolve in the water with the same concentration she brought to bear on all her "personal affairs," that is, all the little things in her life that she took care of herself, with the knowledge and tacit approval of her lover, of course, but it was she who handled them. Her insurance, her taxes, her rent, her doctors' bills — a whole host of details that she had not wanted to foist off on him, or rather on his secretary, despite his repeated offers to handle them for her. She jealously guarded these minor chores as if they were a treasure trove of private details, possessions that she kept from him, thinking that they would only upset or irritate him if he knew about them, whereas in truth he couldn't have cared less.

He watched her now, her pretty neck bent over her glass, staring at the painkillers, which had long since dissolved completely, more attentively, he thought, than she would deal with his own dissolution six months down the road. For her pleasant lifestyle, her regular salary checks, which she found reassuring — even if Paul was paying the lion's share of her expenses — were part and parcel of her dignity, her self-esteem, her personality — in other words, part of the existence of Sonia B., part of its seriousness, therefore part of her health.

Unfortunately, Paul had always thought that women were never more serious than when they were naked. Even if he was aware that Sonia thought of herself as being serious not when she was naked but when she was fully clothed and busying herself with the ways of the world, both socially and professionally, in keeping with the tempo and mores of the time. It was then, and only then, that she felt herself free and responsible. To be sure, Paul did not picture himself, or define who he was, seated on the edge of a bed. But he would have liked a woman to do so in his stead. He would have considered this assessment of himself as accurate as any other.

"Your migraine gone?"

"Not a chance! It's psychological, my doctor says. Any emotional upset, even a minor one, any shock to my system, triggers it immediately. . . ."

"Poor darling! It's all my fault!" Paul said softly, with a saintly smile, his face the picture of devotion and humility, of someone who should have forewarned his mistress.

Unfortunately, Sonia, who was distracted, shrugged her shoulders and murmured: "It's not your fault . . ." which only served to provoke a sudden, uncontrollable wave of rage in Paul. "That's too much," he said to himself, "I mean really too goddamn much!" Not only had he taken away from Sonia his aura of devil-may-care invincibility, not only had he allowed his name to be added to her sad and growing list of recent deaths, what was more, he had had the gall to give her a migraine. . . . Perhaps he owed her an apology for the unseemly shock he had given her, and while he was at it should offer his excuses for his untimely demise.

"Didn't your doctor ever warn you that, when your broken heart was coupled with an intense pain in your brain, there could be dire consequences? That it might lead to unbearable suffering? That you might end up devoid of any worry, any real thought, even any feeling?"

"You've already told me that once," she said. "I know I live like a silly, egotistical, unfeeling goose."

"But I'm not talking about a silly goose, Sonia. You have to admit that when I see you moaning and groaning today about your migraine, whereas six months from now I'll be six feet under . . . well, it makes me wonder, to say the least. Can you understand my . . . my astonishment?"

He felt himself petty, ridiculous, trivial in this unequal battle of comparative pains and sicknesses. Even if he were a thousand times right, so what? She was not devastated by his death; or, rather, her despair gave way to a migraine. And again, so what? Maybe the best thing to do was forget her as soon as humanly possible.

"After all, you're right," he said with a laugh. "Let's cut to the chase: for the time being I feel fine, and you don't. So let's take care of you. Six months from now we'll see."

An expression of concern, verging on spite and fear, had etched itself on Sonia's face, stripping it of all its beauty. At the same time it lent her a new expression, that ambiguous age — from her own to that of her mother — that aggressive acts often inflict on any woman. But Sonia suddenly realized the error of her ways and struck her forehead with her hand — not unlike the heroine of some grade-B movie overemphasizing her feelings — and threw herself into Paul's arms without even taking her painkillers. The clouds disappeared, and she was magically transformed back into the pretty, charming person who had the kindness to give herself body and soul to Paul's every whim and desire.

"My darling," she said, "my great love, you are so right! How could I ever have . . . ? I don't know. . . . I'm so upset I don't know what to do or say in times like this! I'm so afraid of hurting you I'm not sure what to do next. Tell me, sweetheart. You've taught me how to be happy, Paul. Tell me how to act now . . ."

She paused.

"I don't want to teach you now how to be unhappy," he said tenderly. "At least not willingly. On the contrary, I'll do my best to make sure you're not."

It was true that she was doubtless as distraught by the situation as he himself had been earlier in the day. It was possible that his presumed role had seemed to her as false and overwhelming as hers had seemed to him. What right did he have to ask others to be warm and loving and intuitive about him when he was incapable of transcending himself when it came to others? Was there anything so wonderful about somebody who didn't bay at the moon and don sackcloth and ashes? What else had he done that was so amazingly wonderful? Or unique? Poor Sonia! Pretty Sonia! Exquisite Sonia! Sonia who sought refuge in egotism because she was simply incapable of feeling tenderness! This was not an era when people even knew how to be tender: tenderness had been replaced by toughness, and people were exposed to anything and everything — including things they should not have to submit to. Today, nobody knew any longer how to express true feelings. The only thing that mattered was the frenetic, utterly boring pursuit of money; or an apathetic, and sometimes mortal, desire to evade issues. Pleasure itself had become a diabolical danger.

Poor little Sonia, he thought as he folded her in his arms. For she was vulnerable like all little girls, even if they were grown-up and wise in the ways of the world. Poor little Sonia, about whom he had realized not too long ago that what excited him was the fact that she was dumb. Yes, he, Paul-the-kind, Paul-the-decent-guy. No, it wasn't so much her stupidity that aroused him, it was the effect her silliness had on his friends, even the best and the brightest. Their expressions — a combination of sympathy and lust — when Sonia took part in their conversations were meant to embarrass him, but all they did was heighten his desire. However bored he might have been by what he heard her say, he was inevitably aroused by the knowledge of what she was going to do. This banal spice, which was typically bourgeois, this affinity between disdain and desire, was something Paul had discovered early on in his life in the family library. He had not believed in it when he had read it in novels; in fact, he had found the notion revolting. Could you love a woman you didn't respect? Could you worship someone without believing in her? Could you be madly in love with a woman you didn't admire? Well, you could. Not only that, it might be better that way. Easier. It took Paul almost forty years to learn that carnal platitude. Nevertheless, he always took Sonia to dinners where, sooner or later, her stupidity would explode, with the result that brighter souls would inevitably pick up on it right away and cast a sympathetic, albeit ironical, look in his direction, which only excited him all the more.

In his case, perhaps all this was little more than a thinly disguised attempt to disown Helen; or perhaps it stemmed from a natural tendency in men to underestimate women. He had never really given this a great deal of thought. He had simply accepted it. All he knew was that, in his eyes, there was less difference between Sonia's intelligence, or lack thereof, and that of the smartest businessmen he knew than there was between her and some half-smart undergraduate philosophy major. Therein lay the real hierarchy: ten years later — starting at whatever point you chose — what made the difference was what you assimilated along the way, how you fed your mind, not the degree of native intelligence you had to start.

"What do you mean when you say someone's intelligent?" Sonia said in that kind of half-pitched, infantile voice that women over thirty often assume.

"I don't know," he said. "Maybe it means having the greatest number of viewpoints on any given subject . . . being able to see things from several different angles, plus having the capacity to change your mind . . . and to learn. . . ."

"In that case, we learn all the time, since we're forever changing our point of view."

"No, no! The older you become the more you adopt viewpoints that coincide with your own self-interest. Or you don't change your mind at all simply because you've grown lazy. Or you adopt what your peers think or do, or what life at that stage dictates.

As we grow older, our viewpoints shrink and decrease. Inevitably. Little by little we become real jerks. From there we move on to become old farts. At least I will have been spared that awful fate! I'll never have been anything but a young jerk, then a jerk who was well on his way to middle age . . ."

"Stop that," Sonia cried. "I forbid you to say things like that!"

And at long last Sonia did what she should have done from the start: she pulled him to her and smothered him with kisses, first his face, then his neck, then his shoulder, then his hands, paying homage to the life she still felt coursing through him, that rash and sensual life, that life that did not seem for one second in any way consistent with the one his mind had been trying to convince him of for the past six hours.

An hour later, lying on the bed next to Sonia, who was still half asleep, Paul looked at the rug where a ray of sunshine had slipped through the heavy drapes that had been inserted between the afternoon and love. He felt himself there where he ought to be, both for his pleasure and his morale. He was on the narrow ridge between his duty and his rights. He was relaxed, comfortable, distracted, back again in the faithful refuge of his entire life. Very simply, he asked himself, for the first time, what it was that compelled him to count his heartbeats, and the ticks of his watch, and try to establish some sort of relationship or equilibrium between the two — an illogical effort, since he had no fever.

And he also asked himself why he was utterly bored.

Sonia's good-byes were heartrending: he must come back that evening. No? well, tomorrow for sure. "No, I can't wait for tomorrow. Please come back tonight. Just for an hour. Anytime you can make it." As if she didn't trust him, as if he were liable to die before he returned, as if death for her lover were a foregone conclusion — one more in a long line — and he was completely responsible for it.

"Let's not exaggerate," he felt like saying. "After all, I have another six months." But she seemed so determined to make their separation as painful as it was distrustful he didn't have the heart to say no. And since he couldn't bring himself to turn his back to her, he exited by walking backward across the landing toward the stairway, which might easily have resulted in his making a misstep and falling down the stairs, which would have been no big deal given the circumstances, except for the embarrassment. Any minor accident or illness, even a cold, was superfluous, unworthy of so much as a comment. That, too, was something he should constantly bear in mind.

VI

HE LEFT SONIA'S APARTMENT in a far better frame of mind than when he had arrived. In the final analysis, it was better for her, and for himself, that he was not madly in love with her. He only had to think how terrible he would have felt to be separated from Mathilde — when she still loved him — because of something as stupid as an illness. For in such a case cancer would suddenly have ceased to be something both terrible and banal and become an unholy hell, hopelessly cruel and untimely: an obstacle, not a whim of fate. With Sonia he was moving steadily and stoically toward death, whereas with Mathilde he would have desperately wanted to move toward love, and death would have been a dreadful detour. But if on the other hand Mathilde had been taken from him, if she had been the one who had died, that would have been even worse. And for a moment he felt a sense of relief: at least he had been spared the worst.

It was almost five o'clock, and he had an appointment at five-thirty. A business appointment, but between now and then he needed to inform himself more fully about his illness. No question of paying a return visit to this morning's Cassandra. Nor did he have any intention of asking some other doctor out of the blue, who would only prescribe the same tests he had already been given and who, out of a sense of professional ethics, would send him back to his physician of record. No, he would buy a book on the subject. He remembered there was a medical bookstore not far from where he was, in which he found a work entitled *The Various Forms of Carcinoma,* which he purchased only after he had checked with the bookseller and made sure that "carcinoma" was indeed the highfalutin name for cancer. He climbed back into his car and drove over to the Luxembourg Gardens, where he sat down on a bench between two elderly ladies, who were sulking and apparently not speaking to each other, but who now seemed to be sufficiently suspicious of the newcomer in their midst (his hair was mussed, he looked no doubt more than a little distraught) that they closed ranks and left, chirping away like two birds.

Paul began leafing through the book at random, then closed it as soon as he saw that the illustrations were less than reassuring. He opened it again to the table of contents, looking for the chapter on lungs, found it, and read the following first line: "Lung cancer is almost always fatal." He read on as if he were searching for information about somebody else's problem. "The skill and caution required in intrathoracic operative procedures ... etc., etc. requires that only experienced chest surgeons undertake the operation." That flight of medical rhetoric was suddenly interrupted as his book itself took flight, wrenched from his hands by the impact of a soccer ball. Paul scooped up both book and ball and set them beside him on the bench. Looking up, he saw a youngster of nine or ten galloping toward him at full steam, looking incensed if not downright hostile.

"My ball," he said dryly.

"Little jerk," he thought, "and rude to boot."

"I'll give it to you as soon as you say you're sorry," he said firmly.

"Sorry about what?"

"About knocking my book out of my hands."

There was a silence. The child seemed to be completely alone and independent. No maternal voice calling, no friend yelling to find out where he had gone to.

"What are you reading anyway?" he asked.

"A book on carcinoma. In its various forms."

The boy began to circle the bench, repeating in an annoyingly nasal voice: "In its various forms . . . in its various forms . . . in its various forms . . . in its various forms . . . ," hopping on one foot like some kind of cripple or village idiot. Paul looked at him with a mixture of disdain and disgust.

"What's that mean, 'in its various forms'?"

"It doesn't mean you in any case. You're a unique species, called 'total drip,'" Paul said with a self-satisfied snicker, his nasal tone reminding him of the kid's. The illness would be untreatable for a little bastard like him.

And he returned to his book, the soccer ball held firmly under his arm. But he didn't understand a word of what he was reading; the presence of his newfound adversary kept him from concentrating.

"I want my ball!"

"Ask for it politely."

"I don't know how."

The kid was clearly lying. Playing the dead-end kid, the homeless brat, to try to soften up Paul. Well, it wasn't going to work.

"You can try, can't you?" Paul was doing his best not to lose his temper.

"Anyway, you don't have no right to keep the ball. It's not yours to keep. It's my father's, he paid for it!"

"I don't give a good goddamn who bought it."

"I'm gonna get my father."

"Go ahead. And when you bring him back, I'm going to knock his block off," Paul said with conviction.

For a moment the kid stopped in his tracks; an expression of horror and disbelief came over his face.

"No, mister, he's going to knock *your* . . ."

"Think so?" And with that Paul stood up, stretching to his full six feet two and squaring his rugby shoulders for the little monster, who was not only possessive but cowardly to boot.

"Well, shit," the kid managed. "Fact is, my father's not big enough to take you on, that's for sure!"

His outburst calmed Paul down. "Listen," he said, "just say 'I'm sorry' and you can have your ball."

There was a long silence.

"I'm sorry," the kid muttered under his breath.

Paul set the ball down on the ground, aimed, and gave it a kick that send it spinning into the wild blue yonder, while his adversary watched respectfully as it sailed away. Still, Paul could not help thinking, if his

deep thoughts about life and death led him to terror-
ize footloose kids in the ways and byways of public
parks, that was not exactly a good sign either. What
was more, the kid did not look at all terrorized. All he
had done was yield to the demands of an adult, which
had surely done him some good. Paul could picture in
his mind the dinner scene that night as the kid related
his adventure in the park.

"You know, papa, there was this man in the park
today who tried to take my soccer ball away. So I told
him that you had bought it and it belonged to you,
and the man said he didn't give a good goddamn. So I
told him you were going to beat him up and he said
no, he was going to beat you up, and then when he
got up I saw it was true. He would have beaten you
up, papa!"

And as he pictured first the father, then the mother,
Paul broke into a nervous laugh. He realized it was
the first time he had ever used his size and physical
strength to win an argument. Generally he made a
point of doing the opposite, telling stories in which he
was the fall guy, done in by some young whipper-
snapper or other. At first Helen had found it amusing;
then she had found it exasperating. He blamed her for
having changed, but perhaps he should simply have
changed his stories, which lost their spice and humor
in the retelling. It was strange how, since this morning, he kept thinking how much he wanted to remove
the disgruntled mask of the bitter woman from
Helen's face — a mask he had nonetheless endowed
her with over the past few months. As he couldn't
wait to admit that, in the course of their pointless

arguments, he'd been wrong and she had been right. Perhaps, he told himself — and the thought horrified him — perhaps it's because I am going to need her, and because I couldn't bear to be dependent on a woman I didn't admire or didn't love enough. Perhaps — and this was the worst possibility of all — I'm transforming her into a sensitive, wounded woman because I'm afraid that, when the chips are down, she won't help me; and picturing her as a tender, loving woman again reassures me about her reaction as well as about the help she'll give me. Or maybe it was a combination of all the above. Period . . . Am I lying to myself to this extent? he wondered, conveniently forgetting that it was only recently that he had tried, or been forced to, commune a little with himself. Very little.

According to his appointment book, his meeting at five-thirty was with a man who wanted to construct several buildings on the banks of a pond in the near-suburb of Sologne — a spot he happened to know very well. He had been invited there by a friend of Mathilde's, a man who owned a cabin and had years ago leased the hunting rights in the area. Paul had spent several weekends there. Had never fired a single shot, to be sure; Mathilde hated hunting, but they'd both loved these weekends. The cabin, built right over the water and in among the bulrushes, was cozy and warm during those autumn weekends, thanks to an old stove they kept going night and day, and they had spent long hours reading, making love, and eating out of tin cans. He could vividly remember Mathilde's jacket, dark brown with red fur lapels, and her face flushed by the cold. When they came in from outdoors, her face was so bright and icy that when she buried her head in his neck she made him moan with pleasure and cold.

His client had bought these acres, this nice piece of land, which included the pond itself and the cabins around it. He certainly wanted to retain the wild, unspoiled aspect of the place. A great spot for hunting and fishing, but now he would add a touch of class. . . . And with a restaurant, it went without saying, centrally located among the cabins; plus paved roads so you could drive right up to them. And the idiosyncratic showers, which in the old days switched back and forth from hot to cold without warning, would have to give way to proper bathrooms. Ten days ago he had accepted the job with the idea of doing the least damage possible to the environment. Today he didn't give a damn.

Even if he became incapable of taking on any project, he was never going to let anything deprive him of the wonderful stream of images that constantly unfolded in his mind and had for several years, all stemming from the cabin on the pond, without any need for him to call them up: the trees turning gold and russet at nightfall, and the pond, so gray, so smooth, so dark, the anthracite pond; and Mathilde's face glowing in the heat of the stove. . . . While "waiting for Godot" — no, while waiting to die — he was not going to deprive himself of any distraction over the next six months. He wanted to watch time go by, he wanted to savor and welcome it, and it was not by canceling all his appointments that he was going to succeed in that effort. If he had been a great architect, a genius — some latter-day Frank Lloyd Wright or Le Corbusier — the notion of his death might actually have stimulated him, and incited him to bequeath to this planet everything that death was going to take away from him. Perhaps he would have turned out a number of rush jobs — hospitals, palaces, rich men's showplaces, or intimate houses; perhaps he would have invented a whole new architecture, new shapes and forms, something that would have replaced the rabbit warrens that currently housed the poor, or the bizarre stucco constructions that those slightly better off chose as their domiciles. And perhaps, thanks to his creative faculties, he might have managed to transcend himself and forget the destruction of his body.

But he was not a genius in his profession any more than he was in life. In any case, he was less pretentious than those famous cooks or baritones or movie stars whose memoirs and insights are more and more sought after by publishers and clutter up bookstores to the point of nausea. He was a respectable, reasonably talented architect — at least so he had been told in the good old days when architecture seemed to him an art, an art whose primary goal was not financial gain. The word "genius" had disappeared from his vocabulary eons ago . . . disappeared very quietly, in fact, in direct proportion to Paul's ability to solve the questions of "how" in his work, leaving the "whys" not only unanswered but unfaced. Why should he imagine that a writer, or an artist, learning that he had only a short time to live, would feel liberated enough to rush to his pen or his brush and create the scandalous work, or the triumph, that till then he had not felt he could dare attempt? The problem with that was: why had he — or she — not dared try it till now? As for scandal, who in this day and age of total freedom could have fashioned a work that might shock? Would those who revealed their inner secrets be embarrassed? Had life bestowed on them — the talented creators in whatever art form — staggering revelations? Did they think of the chaotic scaffolding of their existence as a superb example that they would toss, like manna from heaven, to a public fascinated by their honesty and distraught by their death? And even if the artist were to say to himself, "Wait a minute! The question before the house is whether or not I'm still capable — as I was when I was fourteen — of giving birth to a masterpiece," the fear of failure, or skepticism about his own talent, would prevent the putative genius from creating anything whatsoever, let alone a masterpiece. The artist, wiser and more acute than ever, would snicker at seeing the work, the pencils and pens, that shoddy paraphernalia, the weary panoply that is supposed to be the mark of genius-at-work, which till now has lain dormant, or fallow, without any great regret. Ah, no! Spare me those speeches in which compassion and confusion mindlessly battle it out! If he were to be judged (and consoled) at all, let it be by women and women alone — for they knew him and he knew them — women who . . . that . . . where is this leading? . . . in short, women who had been his mistresses. Aside from that, no reproaches, no regrets. Even to himself. He had been through too much, heard too much, to take any more, and doubtless given as much as he had got. The six months he had left would not be spent listening to what other people thought or said. Actually, when he thought about it, he didn't listen to others any longer and hadn't for quite some time. Except on those rare occasions when something he was reading caught his attention. It was not that what people were saying was any less interesting; he had simply tuned out. Still, he had to admit that he had admired some people at certain times in his life, creative people in fact, but apparently admiration was a muscle, like intelligence, and if it wasn't used it tended to atrophy. And so you began to be increasingly uninterested, without really noticing it, in those people you saw less and less, in those you listened to or read less and less. What was more, it seemed to Paul that this evolution — this self-leveling, this effort to accept his limitations, this painless shedding of his ambitions and intellectual pleasures — far from bringing him into another circle of friends, less brilliant no doubt but more fun to be with, on the contrary had the nefarious effect of making him lonelier. A loneliness made all the more terrible in that it was, from the start, involuntary, with no compensating up side. Anything, he had decided, no matter how pretentious, no matter what the social situation, would have been preferable to this solitude.

Enough of all that! Let's drink to life! To loneliness! Unfortunately, life for a mortal only too aware of his allotted days was intolerable. How come, he wondered, when the notion of an accidental death did not affect him in the least; in fact, he found it quite bearable. And besides, there were these incredible accidents in which you felt no one would ever come out alive, and yet some came out without a scratch while others were toted off to the morgue. The point was, in an accident you were never sure of the results. Yes, that was it: the idea of imminent mortality could be made bearable, even romantic, if there was an element of doubt about it, an alternative, which gave you the possibility of an out. Made you believe a trifle less in its inevitability. "It's not doubt that drives people crazy, it's certainty that does," Nietzsche said. Or was it someone else? And, man, was Nietzsche right on the mark! What was his first name again? Nietzsche? Nietzsche? Frederick? Ludwig? No, that's not it. Not that it matters, for Chrissake. Who cares what the man's first name was? But nonetheless his mind kept dredging for the answer in the murky waters of his subconscious. Or was it unconscious? Whichever, he came up empty.

He arrived at his office, parked his car in the clearly marked crosswalk, right in the faces of two shocked green-and-purple-outfitted lady cops, whose happy lot in life was to dole out parking tickets. For not only did the car's driver park illegally but he made no effort to slip the necessary parking authorization under his windshield wiper. He then had the gall to walk over to the parking meter, rummage in his pocket for some coins, bend down as if he were listening to the meter, and give it a pat on its little defenseless metal head. And then he had the further gall to walk past them without offering any legal or logical explanation for his bizarre behavior, although there was no way he could not be aware of their presence. The only thing he said, which made no sense but which they duly noted, perhaps out of habit, in their little blue books, was "He's an old pal of mine; he never wants me to pay. I keep trying, and he keeps saying no. Not a damn thing I can do about it!" and with that he disappeared into an office building, which, one may presume, was the site of his professional activities, assuming he still had any.

Paul's refusal to abide by the laws and civil codes of the city, however much a game, had also always been a source of pleasure to him, a pleasure made all the greater by the fact that he had so many parking tickets that he was more than a scofflaw — he was in a category all his own, and he knew that even with their creaky computers they could never catch up with him. Not now, anyway.

He seemed in fine fettle as he walked through the corridors of his office. Before he had arrived he had looked in the elevator mirror at the tall, rugged, dark-haired, strange-looking fellow staring back at him. Objectively, he would never have believed the guy was sick. As the elevator had reached his floor, and just as the door opened, he suddenly remembered Nietzsche's first name: Friedrich. Friedrich Nietzsche! That was it. He gave a sigh of relief, for while he was making fun of his mind search he was also relieved that he would not have to waste another hour or two dredging up the man's first name (for his client, who was already seated in the waiting room, did not look like someone who could provide him with any cultural information, however trivial). Paul made a quick detour to his office to say hello to his longtime, utterly devoted, loving secretary, Irene.

"You're late," she admonished him, "but at least you're looking well."

That stopped him short, and he had a moment's hesitation. But how could he tell Irene his news, his life and death news? In her modest dress and careful chignon, she was too prim and proper, too much a character out of some 1920s novel, for him to think of laying something this heavy on her thin shoulders. No, not Irene; she less than any other woman. Impossible. And the realization that he couldn't tell her made it all the more imperative that he find someone to whom he could reveal the gory details of the hamster's prognosis. And yet he had already told two people, Gaubert and Sonia — three if you count the guy at the gas station — and in all cases he had had the feeling he was playing a role in some comedy. In the first scene he felt he had missed his cue — or perhaps it had been Gaubert, it didn't matter — and the second scene had been too absurd, too ridiculous for any audience, even the audience of one that he represented. No, at this juncture nobody really knew what he knew — maybe because nobody was interested.

"You're right," he repeated mechanically, "and if I look good, it's because I'm feeling good," and for some reason he really didn't fathom he felt pleased with Irene. He gave her a broad smile, and she, shaking her head, responded with her habitual look, half tender, half disapproving. He leaned over so that she could straighten his tie, dust off his jacket, and pull his sleeves down to their proper length. She had been making these same maternal gestures for twelve or thirteen years, and for twelve or thirteen years she had derived the same pleasure from them. He had too, he thought as he straightened up. In addition to these maternal-professional caring gestures, she was also a good secretary, with a mixture of ignorance and intuition that he liked and appreciated.

"Any important information I should know about our client? What's his name again?"

"Pierre Saltiery. Some big wheel in the sports world, I believe. Sports clothes and the undergarments that go with them, I'm told."

Paul wondered what the terms "big wheel" and "undergarments" meant to her. A manufacturer of ski clothes and thermal underwear? Some wheeler-dealer in the world of competitive sports? Or the man behind the slightly risqué Icecapades?

He headed toward his office, stopped to shake Saltiery's hand and lead the way. He sat down on the professional side of the desk. A few hours earlier he had been seated on the other, the bad side.

"Tell me how you got to me?"

That was always his first question. The answer may not have been a hundred percent truthful, but it was inevitably enlightening.

"We've known each other for, oh, twelve, maybe thirteen years," the man said.

That caught Paul's attention, and he looked more closely at the man. He was thin and ruddy, a combination that Paul found slightly disconcerting. He pegged him as a sporting ascetic. Type A. He was wearing a purple corduroy suit, which did not suit him at all well. He was a man, Paul decided, who had not yet made his choice in life — the choice of who he was — and that Paul found reassuring, for he could not help comparing him to this morning's hamster, a man already fixed and frozen in time and space, whose personality was reflected in his professional finery: spotless white coat, carefully controlled voice, his gestures and movements those of a professional underling. No question, Paul loathed this type, quite independently of the man's deadly diagnosis. . . . But what if the hamster had said to him, "All your tests are fine. You're in very good health. Come back and see me in a year?" Would he have hated him just as much? No, but he would never have gone back to see him. On the other hand, he could never have brought himself to hate Dr. Jouffroy, who he knew would have handled the situation with kid gloves. He would have started by telling Paul that he wanted to redo a couple of the tests, they didn't look right the first time, and then he would have said something about Paul's not being quite up to snuff and we'll have to discuss what we're going to do about it. This morning he had felt so helpless, so alone in the presence of the hamster, who (at best) didn't give a damn, or who (at worst) was delighted that a rugged six-foot-two specimen was going to die long before the skinny, five-foot-four pretentious abortion who had somehow, presumably, managed to get through medical school. It was a crying shame: compassion should be an obligatory part of any doctor's education and baggage. They should have a course called Compassion 101. Compassion and all its various implications.

Roughly thirteen years. That would make Paul twenty-six, twenty-seven, at the time. He had not yet made a name for himself, was not very well connected, not very well heeled either. But those were the years when he was still a kid, verging on manhood, and madly in love with a woman who still loved him, or who had already begun to love him less, depending on the month we're referring to in that year.

"We met at Bligny, in fact," Saltiery said. "You came there with Mathilde. I loaned you my cabin on the pond."

So it was he, the man of the cabin. Paul had been jealous of him at the time, but till now he had not remembered his name. Jesus! between his Nietzsche void and completely forgetting Saltiery, no chance of an A in the memory department this week.

"Of course, of course," Paul said, getting to his feet and offering both his hands across the desk to his long-lost client-friend, as if two veterans of the Mathilde campaigns ought to embrace, pat each other on the back, cling to each other as if they were the survivors of some terrible shipwreck — the irreparable happiness that came from having lived with or loved Mathilde. And Saltiery must have felt the same way, because he too got to his feet and took Paul by both arms before sitting back down. His expression was both playful and a mite sad, that of a knowing accomplice, the precise expression that Paul would have liked to have as well.

"What a great spot it was," Paul went on. "Incredibly beautiful. And that's the place you want to . . . change? That's too bad, no? A pity."

"A pity but necessary," Saltiery said. "I bought the whole area a short while ago, including the pond. Bought the land, really, for the hunting cabins had all fallen into rack and ruin. So I have no choice but to rebuild. It will still be a hunting preserve, but catering to the . . . how shall I say . . . to the urban wealthy. Snobs if you prefer. Places for duck hunting. Bungalow-style buildings, set far enough apart so people have their privacy. Living room, one or two bedrooms, and a kitchen big enough to eat in. You know, American style. The kind of duck-hunting lodge people of this kind deserve."

"I see you have as high regard for contemporary architecture as I do," Paul said with a laugh. And he reached across the desk and handed him a cigar, a mark of esteem and also a sign to his fellow architects, should he summon one or more of them in, that this was a serious new client who should be treated with deference.

"I've already given some thought to your project," Paul said regretfully. "My approach was to do as little damage as possible. All of which of course depends on what kind of material you envisage, what size and shape you see the buildings, and how many you want to construct."

All of a sudden he was relaxed, focused, curious. All of a sudden he wanted to turn this superb area into something absolutely wonderful. As romantic and seductive as he remembered it as a young man madly in love thirteen years ago. Or was it twelve? It was someone like Saltiery he would have needed to confide in rather than a guy like Gaubert.

"In fact, I've already made some preliminary sketches," he said. "Here, let me show you."

And he opened his drawer, pulled out a bunch of drawers, and tossed them pell-mell onto the top of the desk, thus violating all the unwritten rules of his profession, which obliged an architect to display the fruits of his or her imagination sketch after sketch, slowly and in a specified order, and to do that only when the contracts had been signed or virtually signed. But there they were, all the creative ideas and plans and drawings that Paul's imagination and training had come up with. Work that the gentleman across the desk, if he so desired and was not in good faith, could easily visualize and pilfer for his own ends.

But today what did that matter? Everything seemed light and inconsequential to Paul; since there was no future, there was no continuity. In a way that made life easier, knowing your every act was gratuitous or, rather, knowing life would soon be over. There was no longer anything to exploit, to keep, to make use of. Nothing was any longer salable, productive, or positive. Interesting: these words had always rung hollow to him as far back as he could remember. At long last he felt he could offer himself, or his work, without regard for the amount of effort that had gone into it or the financial gain he or his firm would derive from it. The truth was, his life had taken on a whole new dimension, a value system that till now had been sorely lacking. Not only lacking in him, he thought, but in his entire generation, maybe throughout the world.

"Television," Saltiery was saying, waving his large, bony hands for emphasis. "I want each bungalow to be equipped not only with a television set but also a VCR." He saw that Paul was eyeing him warily, so he hastened to explain: "I'll equip each cabin — excuse me, each bungalow — with a pile of films with a hunting plot — Gregory Peck just before he's torn to pieces by a tiger, Robert Redford" — quickly updating his film stars to show he was of the Redford rather than the Peck generation — "setting free the elephants, that kind of thing."

Paul wasn't quite sure he got the point but he held his tongue, suspecting the rationale would follow.

"These weekend hunters," Saltiery went on, "they'll leave a wake-up call for four A.M. so they can go shoot some ducks. But worn-out as they'll be by their nighttime frolics with their mistresses or girl-friends, they'll all roll over at four A.M. and go back to sleep. So they won't get to shoot any ducks, but they'll come away from the weekends filled with hunting action thanks to the VCR and, believe me, they'll think they've had a great weekend."

"I can see that you're not exactly crazy about your customers either."

"For ten years I've been catering to these rich and famous assholes," Saltiery said, shrugging his shoulders. "What can I tell you, it's a living. A good living in fact. What I've learned is that the more vulgar my projects are, the more they cater to the herd instinct, the better they work. That is, assuming my groups all come from the same income bracket . . ."

No way I'm going to finish my career in a sado-masochistic project such as this, Paul said to himself. But the guy is more than half decent. Slightly bitter, but a nice enough sort.

"What kind of buildings would you put up if you really liked your customers?" Paul asked. "The kind of primitive cabins that were there before?"

"Hell, no! I hated that spot, and I'll tell you why. I used to lend the cabin you know to Mathilde for the weekend, with no strings attached. I was hoping of course she might reward my generosity by spending one of her weekends with me. But of course that was not to be: she always showed up with a rugged, well-built guy, the same guy weekend after weekend. But I don't have to tell you. . . . Anyway, after you two broke up I still had high hopes she might give me the nod. But not for long . . ."

"Why, did she show up with someone else?"

"No, she simply returned me the keys and said she wouldn't be needing the place anymore. She's a sensitive soul, but she's got the willpower of a mule."

Speaking of Mathilde in the present bothered Paul almost as much as hearing the hamster doctor talk about him in the past.

"You have any idea what's become of her? I know she moved out of her old place. . . ."

"Yes. She still lives on the rue de Tournon, up near the Senate. It's a door or two from the building that has that famous café on the ground floor, you know the one, the café where all those expatriate Americans and Brits from *Merlin* and the *Paris Review* used to hang out after the war."

"Long before my time," Paul murmured. "But I go there a lot."

"Long before my time, too," Saltiery said, not wanting to be outdone in the age war. "Anyway, she married some rich English guy. Then divorced him. I see her once in a while. Every three months or so we have lunch together."

"How is she?

"Beautiful. As beautiful as ever. Anyway, that's the way I see her. You see, I've never had her, and a woman you haven't gone to bed with always retains a certain attraction, don't you agree?"

"I wouldn't know," Paul said, then caught himself. "I don't mean to say that I've had every woman I desired," he said, "but I've always chosen women who liked me from the start. Maybe it simply means I'm lazy. Or that I prefer to take the low road to happiness. Or maybe I'm just the cautious type. I don't know."

All of which was true, though in fact he'd never given it any thought till now. Strange, no? As if he were only aroused by what he knew he could have. What did that mean? Maybe he should ask Saltiery, who seemed to be a pretty sharp guy. He would have liked to open up to him. Say to him: "Look, I'm going to die. What do you think I should do about it? What would you do if you were in my shoes?" But of course he didn't. He couldn't. This poor guy, he's clearly already had it up to here with his boring profession —

one that in any event seems to bore him out of his mind — does he need my heavy-duty problems to boot? Obviously not. Besides, he, Paul, already had a close friend, the one and only Robert Gaubert. They didn't come any better. A bosom buddy. All heart. And despite himself he began to laugh sarcastically, much to Saltiery's surprise.

"I've decided not to take on your project," Paul said. "I like you a lot, but I'd like to take on a project my client really likes. Does that make any sense?"

"All sorts of sense," Saltiery said, which endeared him to Paul even more. "I confess that I only wish I liked my own project more myself . . . what can I say? Maybe next time, when I come up with something really fun or interesting or difficult I'll give you a call. . . . By the way, I really liked that motel you built in Barbizon a lot. It really turned me on."

They parted on the friendliest of terms, but all Paul could think as he escorted Saltiery to the door was that he would never see him again. The thought saddened him, and he realized that his new mind-set had also made meeting Saltiery all the more poignant.

Stepping back into his office, he saw on his notepad Mathilde's phone number, which Saltiery had scribbled there. But his own phone was ringing. It was Gaubert, Irene told him, adding that he had already called five times. "I'm sorry, but I forgot to tell you," she added, without a trace of remorse, for (he already knew) she detested Gaubert, whom she found "brutal and heartless," whereas he, Paul, considered him no more than awkward and secretive. In any case, he did not take this sixth call, which seemed to delight Irene.

He now realized that he had always had a slight superiority complex vis-à-vis Gaubert, but that their meeting this morning — or was it this noon? — had masked it with a sarcastic indifference or, rather, unmasked it, stripping it of all affection, all esteem. Their relationship, thus laid bare, seen in the cold, harsh light of reality, simply was nonexistent. Even assuming that he was ever truly part of my life, Paul mused, it is safe to say that as of this morning he's out of it. Gone! And that was fine as far as Paul was concerned, since he would shortly be out of his own life as well. The fact was this condensed magazine entitled *The Life and Death of Paul Cazavel* would leave behind no mourners.

Meanwhile, he continued to be amazed by how perceptive Irene was. She was blessed with the kind of intuitive powers granted only to secretaries who have lived with (and been in love with, to be sure) their bosses. Still, it was astonishing to see, as one grew older — no, as one inched slowly toward adulthood — how accurate clichés and proverbs were.

The back of his mind was beset by a flood of quick, cold — and insignificant — thoughts, flitting to and fro as they damn well pleased, without his paying them much heed, since all the foreground of his mind could really think about was the eight figures on his notepad that made up Mathilde's phone number. The phone number of today's Mathilde; the living, breathing Mathilde; Mathilde who lived on the rue de

Tournon not far from the famous — or infamous — literary café that he knew like the back of his hand; Mathilde who till recently he had thought lived at the other end of the world, or in any case "somewhere else": for he could not have long endured the thought that she lived close by and was living without him. As he would not have been able to put up with the idea that she was available to him — at least in his mind. Because these figures that stared up at him from the corner of his desk, which were the road leading to her, were especially seductive: a telephone number with three 4's, two 0's, and three 8's. A well-orchestrated, harmonious phone number, like everything she touched. Because he already knew the number by heart: 48-00-48-84. The number of his great love. Because he could remember her old number, too, the number in his time, his number in fact; 229-29-92, as he remembered how much these neutral numbers were exotic to him. They had a pleasant echo to them; they were lucky numbers, almost sensual. Because Mathilde's street had been Bellechasse, and her exchange the stunning "Babylon." Exchange: how exotic that notion seemed today, when all the old names had been wiped away as if they had never existed. Yes, it was high time that he, Paul, left his fellow creatures behind, left behind the slow, dismal distraction of the planet that he saw taking place inexorably every day. Not to mention the extinction of the best and the brightest of his generation.

While he was on his latest nostalgia trip, he began calling up in his mind the names that in his youth had been given to the various telephone areas of the city.

The postal authorities — sorry, the telecommunications conglomerate — had killed off Carnot, Danton, Macmahon, and Kleber, all heroes in their own right, as they had swallowed up the Pyramids, the Pyrénées, and Wagram. And how could you not love someone whose telephone number began with Jasmin? For consolation, all the telecommunications thugs came up with was the number 4. And then he thought: Good God, all that is going to be taken away from me. Life will go on without me. People will exchange phone numbers — even if they're no longer exotic and poetic — and words of love. New inventions will come to replace the old, new inventions of which I'll never be aware. Life will go on, people will laugh, call each other, fall in love. . . . Without me?

Without him? They would live without him? Irene would go on without him, would fight her way into the city, walk across the Paris bridges he loved so much. Late to work as usual . . . And all this would go on with him ensconced in a wooden box. Alone, cold, slowly turning to dust . . . It was unthinkable . . . un-bear-able . . .

Again, the horror of it all caused him to slump into an easy chair, his body still, his hands gripping each other tightly in front of him like some old man. No! No? . . . This had to stop, somehow he had to get this idea out of his head or else he'd have to start taking tranquilizers nonstop till the end. It was just too impossible . . . and he moaned out loud as a wave of revolt, of refusal, flowed over him and enveloped him in its banality, its cruelty, unbreakable and insipid. . . .

He take tranquilizers? You mean, like Sonia's

girlfriend? Thanks but no thanks. Better resort to the trusty old rifle. As a matter of fact, he had seen a number of people in the last stages of cancer, and fear was among the least of their concerns. For they no longer believed in their own death. Their minds refused to accept it: the imagination was too lively, memory too vivid, the heart too vulnerable to look death straight in the eye, challenge the dark hole, the yawning void, that lay before them. . . . He'd doubtless do the same: like them he would pretend it was not going to happen. And however humiliating the notion of his intelligence forsaking him, of panic besetting him, he could not imagine holding his weakness in contempt. To be sure, he had never been as indulgent, as debonair with himself: but then on the other hand his life had never been very tough, either.

The wave of horror had receded now but was, he knew, lurking there somewhere: behind his back, in front of him, outside, in the distance, in any case biding its time, waiting to return. And his mind was poised to flee. . . . Anything, anybody, any tranquilizer, any dose of morphine, any kindly doctor however sly or slippery, any doctor however conniving and moneygrubbing — whatever it might take to get the job done — books, credulousness, goodness, interest, sadism, anything and anybody will be welcome. Anything that would help him forget, help him escape, make him love or laugh. Anything and everything that might offer him a minute's peace, give him back again his old zest for life, provide even a smidgen of courage (not that he'd ever had very much). He would grab and hang on to the slightest desire, the dimmest memory, the barely remembered refrain of jazz, he would focus on them as if they were so many lighthouses pointing the way, as if they were the quiet bays and backwaters where, after the terrible tempest had abated, the few surviving ships would go to tie up.

VII

IT WAS PAST SIX O'CLOCK, and the evening breeze, filled with the smell of earth and rain, a chill breeze that carried with it the smell of woodsmoke and gas — in short, the smell of Paris — seeped in through the half-open office window. Paul took deep breaths, gulped the air down as a thirsty person gulps down water; his head was still thrown back, his long legs stretched out in front of him; below his rolled-up sleeves his arms dangled down from the sides of his easy chair. He must look as if he were already dead, he said to himself; and the deep-blue veins that ran like so many tiny canals the length of his arms, still tan from the summer sun — this deceitful evidence of his health and vitality reminded him of a child's drawings. And the sight also filled him with a slight feeling of disgust.

The gusts of wind and their attendant odors came and went, flooding him by slow degrees with a new feeling that was neither horror nor vertigo; nor was it the refusal to accept the situation. No, it was on the contrary a premature feeling of sadness, of overwhelming regret for his planet. The planet earth, whose seasons he had known and savored, earth with its verdant grass, its glorious sunsets, its foaming, bright blue seas . . . this earth, friendly even in the fall when its warm rains turned the world gray, even during the winter's coldest days, its days of snow when it showed itself at its most fragile. Everything about this world he had discovered in the course of his childhood and youth was going to be taken from him — not taken, wrenched. This still bright and beautiful world, which man, despite all his efforts, had still not managed to ruin. This abundant, swarming planet, filled with all manner of fauna — faithful, naïve animals that helped you put up with your fellow man, or helped you ignore him. A dog! For months he had wanted to buy a dog, but he had kept on putting it off. Each time he had mentioned it to Helen she had resisted: can you imagine what a dog would do to my furniture? Not to mention these rugs! But now there was no point: why buy a dog, which would probably become his best friend, if he was going to leave it bereft a few short months later — probably just as the dog had grown to love him? A dog that would suffer because of Paul, who would be living a dog's life. No, would die like a dog. That's not funny, Paul. . . . He should have made up his mind sooner. If he had, if he had bought a dog, he'd have someone to confide in and commiserate with now, plus the sure knowledge that the animal would truly miss him. Whether it was a two-legged or four-legged earthling mattered little. Just so there was some creature who cared.

They'd never had a child. It was Helen's fault, though she didn't know it. When she didn't get pregnant, she suggested they both have fertility tests, but he adamantly refused, claiming the tests were too humiliating but knowing that the problem was hers, that she'd be devastated when she found out. Paul knew he was fertile because he already had a child, a little girl who looked so much like him he couldn't bear to see her. He'd carefully refrained from telling Helen, who as a result constantly blamed him for her not being able to get pregnant, for the fact they'd always be alone.

"Is there anything more I can do?"

Irene's silhouette was in the doorway, and at first Paul couldn't fathom who she was or what she wanted. Her discretion was such that he almost hadn't heard her, and then he realized that she must have seen him stretched out here and mistaken his indulgent daydreaming, his wallowing inner monologue, for an act of creation. QUIET: GENIUS AT WORK. DO NOT DISTURB. If only she knew!

"If not I'll be going. I didn't want to disturb you."

He saw her face now, topped by her pert little scarf, and it was the epitome of respect, understanding, and confidence. She put her forefinger to her lips, waved a modest good-bye with her other hand, and tiptoed out.

The wind had risen, and the office shutters were banging noisily. Paul got to his feet, pushing his daydreams into the background, as if he had been called to order. And he knew clearly in his own mind what the next order of the day was: he was going to see Mathilde. Mathilde was the only one who could deal with the situation openly, honestly, positively. Not with a grim face but with a smile. He was deathly afraid, he kept telling himself, that she might refuse to see him, or worse yet agree to see him and then send him packing. But the truth was he was afraid she might not any longer be the same Mathilde he'd known and loved. He was afraid that when he saw her again he might discover another Mathilde, a side of her that had perhaps always been there — a vulgar, vain, or stupid side — to which he had been blinded by love. In other words, he'd discover that his great love story was only an egotistical projection of his own making. For when all was said and done, who was responsible for all the disappointments he had suffered in the course of the day? All those cruel, unsatisfied faces, both those who had made an effort to comprehend and those who had turned a deaf ear: they were, after all, the faces of his life, faces that belonged to people he had always considered near and dear to him. Of the three closest, he was forever hurting Helen, constantly using Robert, and taking pleasure from Sonia. Nothing very deep there. No, there was no question that Mathilde was the only person in his life who was generous enough, and disinterested enough, to see him and deal with him as he was. His real self: and he needed to make sure he had a clear image of his real self to present to Saint Peter at the pearly gates, if in fact the old bearded one was really there to greet him. And the question was, the burning question: would the Mathilde of today coincide with, live up to, his memory of the Mathilde of yesteryear?

The fact that a woman you love reaches a point in the relationship where she ceases to love you, and despite that you can never bring yourself to scorn or de-

spise her, is very rare indeed. And yet wouldn't it have
been better if, when they had broken up, she had
poured a little salt in their wounds, made their parting ugly rather than kind, thus preventing her victim
from forever seeing their affair through rose-colored
glasses, making any future relationship pale by com-
parison? But whether Mathilde had acted like an
angel or a bitch when they had broken up interested
Paul not one iota now, anymore than it had at the
time. What obsessed him was the fear that she might
have grown old, that she might have gone downhill,
lost it (that indefinable "it"), that instead of desiring
and admiring her as he always had, instead of having
complete confidence in her judgments and opinions,
he might end up pitying her. He could not bear the
thought of feeling sorry for Mathilde. That would be
just too much: on top of his loveless marriage, his uncaring friends, the stupidity of his mistress, the use-
lessness of his work, not to mention the imminence of
his death and the awful pain that was bound to go
with it, if in addition the sainted memory of his one
true love were to go down the tube or out the window
or whatever the expression was, then death would not
only be deserved but welcome. None too soon. My
God, what a distressing effect this morning's news
was having on him; not only distressing but deplorable, perhaps unfair. In the course of no more
than a few hours he had, in drawing up the balance
sheet of his days, come up with nothing but deficits
and personal shortcomings: he who no less than
twelve hours earlier would, if asked, have traced the
trajectory of his life as a rising curve, the life he had

willfully chosen, as he would have described himself as a reasonably happy man, who, if not at the peak of his existence, was still sufficiently blessed on so many fronts that peaks and valleys did not concern him.

How wrong he had been all this time! But then, what person, however powerful or wretched, had not woken up at least once in his or her life and pondered — in a state of inexplicable terror — the precarious nature of things, the fragility of oneself and one's world, the inevitability of death? What human being, born of woman, come into this world by chance, under the best of circumstances a child wanted by both father and mother, has not been terrified at the notion of how dependent his life and fate are on his meager abilities, both physical and mental, so that he dreams of having been endowed with other, greater gifts to cope with the problems of the world? No question . . . That is, you know you're going to die one day, it's only a question of when, so what's the big deal? No, that's not right either. In your mind you've learned to live with death — that's a funny expression, no? — but you always think of it in the future, not something you worry about in the present. The sting, the pain, was to die immediately. Now. That didn't go down, not at all. But what could he do about it? Not a damn thing. Which was no good either. Just because he was now going to die before his allotted time was no reason to get so wrought up. As long as he'd assumed he was going to die later on, granted his biblical three score and ten, he'd been a happy man. A happy object. An object that had accepted its condition as object. That had accepted the relatively low esteem in which it was held by its so-called inner circle. And he had accepted whatever had come his way with verve, passion, gratitude. Despite everything. Because of everything. It was imperative he become that happy object again, or his entire life would have been in vain. He would not even have had a life. It was a question of honor. A matter of life and death.

It was only after he got outside that he remembered the reason he had come there was to draw up a list of his various projects and plans and determine who among his colleagues he was going to assign to each. He had meant to be a complete professional, and he had ended up spending all his time with Mathilde's ex-suitor. Strange, their conversation, yet he had somehow enjoyed it. And it had produced Mathilde's current phone number, which struck him as being the only positive element the day had brought him thus far.

Paul got into his car, which, especially after this evening's wind, smelled of tobacco and paper — that special paper odor that clings to architectural draw-ings — his odor, in short. And suddenly Paul realized that this was the only place on the face of the earth that was his. The apartment, with its flowers and fur-niture and sandalwood air freshener, was Helen's and Helen's alone: she ruled over it as a queen her king-dom. Those four walls, which for most men meant a refuge from the slings and arrows of the outside world, did not belong to him. His home was definitely not his castle. No, the only thing that was truly his was this iron monster, this beast with a powerful engine, this map-filled, cigarette-butt-infested site, and for the first time in his life he understood those automobile nuts who were ready to do battle — armed only with their hydraulic jacks — with anyone who might dent or disturb their precious machines, their shelters, their only refuges.

And he began to hum to himself, with great conviction: "My only refuge. My dear sweet refuge! The refuge of my nights, the refuge of my life!" Didn't quite rhyme but what the hell. He was stopped at a red light, and as had happened earlier in the day he looked over at the driver next to him in the car to his left, and saw that the man was staring at him with an air of deep concern. And Paul, as if he were one of those slightly aging jazz buffs you constantly run into in Paris, began to tap out a beat with his hands on the steering wheel, to the tune of some song the driver unfortunately could not hear but which he had to assume was wild and crazy. In fact, Paul's lyrics consisted of: "My refuge, that's my refuge, the refuge of all my days," sung to the tune of "Night and Day." He must have appeared even more demented than when the driver had first seen him, but now that he had pegged him as an aging jazz buff, he looked less worried. When the light turned green, Paul let the man in the car to his left pass him, and he saw that the worried frown on his face had disappeared. No, he was not crazy, and he could prove it. Prove it to whom? To what? This driver, this witness to his presumed dementia, looked like a complete idiot when his mouth was closed. What would the guy look like

if, God forbid, his mouth was open? Did that mean
that each time one of the world's imbeciles gave him a
dirty or even inquiring look he was going to have to
try to act normal, in perfect health, thank you very
much? The way this morning he had played tough
guy, don't worry about me, Mac, to the hamster? Was
he going to spend the rest of his life — what little
remained — walking around with head high and stiff
upper lip, to the admiration of one and all? Hell, no!
He had spent far too much of his life kowtowing
to the rules and regulations, the customs and mores of
the world, for him to add insult to injury by playing
the role of hero in the face of death. . . . Playing it for
whom? It was true that you end up being the person
you mimic, and that you perhaps become insensitive
and invulnerable as a result of pretending to be what
you're not. He would do his best to be upbeat, light,
and uncaring. For others, out of a sense of modesty
and decency, and above all for his own self-esteem.
But when he was alone, when he was with people he
didn't know? Then he would let himself go as much
as he wanted: he would whine and whimper to his
heart's content in public if he wanted to. Even on café
terraces if he damn well felt like it. He owed the world
nothing. He owed nothing to anyone. The thought of
his local tax collector brought a snicker to his lips.
The poor bastard would have a long wait this year before he could dig into the pockets of the recently departed Paul Cazavel. Winding sheets have no pockets.
Another positive thought.

On that subject, how would they bury him, in a
winding sheet or a three-piece suit? What did the law

say on that score? What did they usually do? How did all that work? Was he supposed to order his own casket? Before the "event"? Couldn't very well do it after, now could he? That wasn't funny either. And what about the music for the funeral mass? Should it be Verdi's *Requiem?* Or a piece of Schubert chamber music? Maybe Schumann, he really loved Schumann. He pulled up in front of a music store and bought a tape of Verdi's *Requiem,* which he slipped in the car stereo in place of Tina Turner. He really had a hard time picturing himself dead. What if he pulled out all the stops and spent a fortune on his funeral? Went to the choicest, highest-priced casket maker and ordered the top of the line? Or maybe he should simply opt to be cremated. No, cremation would be too painful for the already weeping throng, he was sure. He'd already gone through that, though on the other end, so to speak. And besides, why not give back to the good earth a bit of what it has given you all these years (not that many, really)? Let the insects and plants and roots nibble away to their heart's content at his carcass. It was simpler, more natural, more . . . more earthly. Paul loved the land and all those that worked it, though when he thought about it he had no peasant roots and absolutely no knowledge of how the earth brought forth its boundless treasures.

VIII

THE RUE DE TOURNON, still bathed in sunlight, though only precariously, seemed more deserted than usual. It was a street that had always struck him as a movie set, circa 1943, a street on the verge of being invaded by a swarm of black-helmeted soldiers, and on which lived only men who were either reckless or fully aware of what was about to happen. It also reminded him of a street in the provinces, with solid, handsome eighteenth-century buildings lining either side in perfect harmony, a street down which, like some kind of dubious anachronism, the staid senators in their stately cars appeared sporadically.

Back now in present time, Paul saw a gendarme appear from his guardhouse to greet a large black sedan, doubtless bearing one of the august members of the Senate, and motion him into the inner sanctum before returning stiffly to his post like some windup soldier. The perfect alignment of buildings was interrupted only by the café near the top of the street, where four tables and ten chairs flowered in front of its windows each summer. It was a quiet street, perhaps too quiet for the impulsive Mathilde, he thought, but then he corrected himself, remembering how much she liked to hobnob and chew the fat with the local merchants, and then he pictured her emerging from her apartment in the morning in her housecoat, going out to buy her bread and croissants. And maybe it was right for her, too, because he could also picture her on such a street as this, reading beside the fire. Despite her flair and her occasional need for flamboyance, Mathilde was someone who hated noise.

Paul entered the café and took a table by the window. He eyed the telephone perched on the gleaming silver counter. He would have preferred not to call her, but to confront her suddenly face to face without any prior warning. The expression in her eyes, before she had had a chance to think, was more important to him than any words.

But in addition to the fact that he had almost never showed up at anyone's place without calling ahead, and that this precept was more ingrained in him than many others that were presumably more important, the hard fact was he didn't know her exact address. His heart was pounding, and despite the Perrier he had just downed, his throat was parched as he stood at the counter and dialed her number. Through the café window with its matching curtains that draped each side he saw a stray dog on the far sidewalk, not far from an old man who looked just as lost as the dog. Finally both crossed the street, treading carefully between the implanted metal markings of the crosswalk, and went their separate ways as soon as they had safely reached the other side. The telephone had rung a number of times without an answer, but Paul remembered — among the thousands of details about her that had been flooding back — that she was often in the habit of not answering the phone until its ringing became unbearable. Suddenly somebody did pick up the receiver.

"Yes?" said a low, throaty, very young voice.

Mathilde's voice.

"It's me," he blurted out.

Good God, what a great start! What did he think he was doing? Why was he bothering her? What right did he have to resurface in the life of this woman who had deserted him a decade before? To announce that he was going to die in the very near future? Impertinent. Pretentious.

"It's me," he said again. "It's me, Paul."

"Paul . . ." she echoed. "Where are you?"

"Right next door. At the rue de Tournon café as a matter of fact . . . Uh, I'd like very much to talk to you if you have a minute. . . ."

"I live at number twelve," she said quietly, as if it were the most natural thing in the world to have heard from him. "On the ground floor, at the end of the courtyard. Give me fifteen minutes, okay? Then ring."

She hung up, leaving Paul completely nonplussed, as if he had never really believed he would ever see her again. He had to think up something to say, some reason for calling out of the blue. But now that he was going to see her, he sure as hell didn't intend to lay his heavy tale of woe on her. Maybe she was married. No, Saltiery said she was divorced. In any case, she was living with someone. Maybe she imagined her old flame was trying to crawl back into her life. No, no way he could tell her the truth. What right, after ten years, did he have to show up and greet her with "Hey, guess what? I'm going to die!" That was no concern of hers. For ages their lives had been parallel and distant. She would only be shocked and exasperated at seeing this big hulk of a man, whom she probably remembered as a gawky boy, emerge out of the past brandishing his death as if it were an identity card. How could he even imagine doing such a thing?

Fifteen minutes. He looked at his watch: only a minute had passed since he had hung up. God, how time was dragging. In contrast with the way it had been flying since this morning. Flowers. Yes, he should show up with some flowers. There was a flower shop a couple of blocks away, down near the Odéon, which as he remembered sold nothing but roses. The best roses in town. He hurried down the rue de Tournon, bought an armload of pale pink roses at the peak of their beauty — maybe a smidgen beyond — that would have done any church proud. They smelled as good as they looked.

That whole errand had taken him all of nine minutes. He felt flushed and transparent, like some awkward kid in the throes of puppy love, and as he hurried back up the street he avoided the quizzical looks of the passersby, who, thank God, were mercifully few. He didn't go back to the café, though his throat was still as dry as sand. He was more afraid of seeing Mathilde again, he realized, than dying of cancer in six months. Throughout his life he had always given preference to aesthetics and true feelings over material gain, which had caused him his fair share of problems. He thought of his relationship with Helen, and realized that she had never been able to understand how one could be smitten with a sudden, spontaneous carnal desire, as she failed totally to comprehend how his excitement over some new architectural project could blind him to the realities of the wily ways of dishonest contractors.

Meanwhile, in the course of his errand to buy the roses he had looked for and located number twelve, a solid, handsome eighteenth-century building just like its neighbors. Ah, fifteen minutes exactly. He opened the porte cochère and noted the courtyard, which had to date back a good two centuries, from the look of its uneven cobblestones. In the middle of the courtyard stood a single tree, which struck him as incongruous and slightly funny. He hurried across the courtyard, stopped in front of her door, and rang. It was as if the movement from the porte cochère to her apartment door had been made in the blink of an eye. The door was opened, and there was Mathilde, unchanged, he thought with an inner sigh of relief as he took her in his arms, unless it was she who took him in hers.

I'm back, he said to himself, I came back. And then he was overwhelmed by a feeling of immense relief, the first he had felt all day, and he closed his eyes.

She drew him inside, and then with a quick, deft maneuver that he remembered she often used to make when she thought she was not at her best, turned him around so that he was in the light and she had the light behind her. He made no effort to resist.

She was wearing a long garnet-red dressing gown with a sable collar, which accentuated her high cheekbones, her luminous, almond-shaped eyes, and the fullness of her lips. She was, he thought, a wonderful mixture of today's woman and a woman of yore, a fully liberated woman who was yet completely romantic. A woman with so many contradictory — no, overlapping — qualities that she could seduce anyone on the face of the earth. There was no way in the world he could, or even should, talk about his problem with Mathilde, tell her the truth. He needed to make a good impression on her, period. But he was also fully aware that the new Paul, today's Paul, Paul-the-condemned, would have a very hard time holding it back, keeping the truth from the one person he had ever loved, telling her how little time he had left. . . .

"As handsome as ever!" she said with a silver laugh, eyeing him shamelessly.

"I've aged," he said, "well, to some degree anyway."

"Yes," she said, still smiling, "there, and there . . . and there . . ." touching with her finger first his forehead, then his cheeks, then the corner of his mouth. "That's called maturity," she said, "at least for men. With women, as you well know, maturity takes on a whole other meaning."

"You haven't changed a bit," he said, and meant it.

She laughed and took him by the hand. "Come, have a seat. Over here by the window. For despite your kind words I *have* aged. In case you've forgotten, you were seven years younger than me. And still are. So do your arithmetic."

"You're just as beautiful as ever. And just as seductive. Which I'm sure you still put to good use," he added with a touch of bitterness, which made them both laugh.

"Good God," he thought, this woman was my wife, my life companion. He looked over at her and realized that that was what she was. Nothing less. And he was her life companion, too. He should never have accepted their separation. Even his impending death seemed secondary to him in the light of that realization. Yes, he had had a reason for living. He had *nonetheless* had a reason for living! And at the same time that he was overcome with a feeling of enormous relief, of complete happiness, he suddenly and without warning broke out in a series of uncontrollable sobs, so violent that he found himself doubled over in his chair, before the astonished eyes of Mathilde, who had no idea what was happening.

"I'm sorry," he stammered, "Jesus, I'm so sorry. But the reason I had to see you, the reason I came here is that . . . you're the only person I can talk to about this . . . you know, you're the only woman I've ever loved . . . what I'm trying to say is that I've got this thing on my lungs that . . . Six months, the doctor tells me I have only six months to live."

By now he had managed, he didn't remember how, to cross the room and was seated on the floor beside her, his head on Mathilde's lap. "And all that shit out there . . ." He gestured toward the street, toward the world beyond the window, his tone one of pain, of deep distress. He was holding his head in his hands, trying to hide the flow of tears, and Mathilde's face was bent over him, as her lips touched his flooded fingers and probed to reach the face beyond.

"My poor darling," she whispered. "My poor sweet man. Tell me how you feel. Unhappy? Afraid? Does it hurt? Tell me, are you suffering? Are you sure you're not suffering? My darling, darling man. Is there someone who's helping you? How long have you known? And who have you told this to? Anyone? You should have come and seen me the minute you knew. . . ."

"Since this morning," he stammered. "And ever since it's been sheer hell. The only ones I've told are . . . oh, two idiots," he finished, having made up his mind that he would spare her the knowledge that the "two idiots" were none other than his mistress-of-the-moment, who had reacted coldly and artificially and self-centeredly (if that was a word), nothing at all like Mathilde's immediate, caring response; and his best friend, who it turned out was far more interested in his telephone calls than in his putative friend. Neither one, after ten years of so-called love on the one hand and so-called friendship on the other, had been able to come close to matching Mathilde's reaction after ten years of separation. Oh, yes, how right he had been to fall in love with Mathilde. And how wrong he had been to drop her (he was conveniently forgetting, caught up as he was in the sea of her endless virtues, that it was she who had dropped him). He had been crazy to live without her all these years, on this empty, bitter earth. He loathed his stupidity. He gave a deep sigh, almost a moan, and was surprised to hear himself. And he thought that this must have been the umpteenth time he had either let himself go — as he had at the memory of the near-fatal mishap at the Evry racetrack — or repressed a wave of anger and self-pity, as he had at the gas station, and wondered if this was going to become a continuing pattern. Even now, in this neat little living room, which had welcomed him, he was acting like a scared, spoiled kid. Out of control, for God's sake. Where was his self-esteem? He was momentarily reassured by Mathilde's reaction, by her very presence, and at the same time he was completely ashamed of his own reaction. The way he saw things at the moment, Mathilde was going to take care of everything; Mathilde would take care of him. Mathilde was going to do everything, or nothing, it mattered little, the point being that she would be with him to help him face the grim reaper.

"What about your wife?" the voice above him was saying. "I understood you got married."

"I haven't told her yet. In all fairness, I haven't seen her yet today, at least since I got the news."

"You mean you couldn't call her? You must have known how to reach her by phone, no?"

Mathilde broke off. She had no idea what Paul's relations with his wife were, and preferred to leave it that way.

"Here," she said, taking a handkerchief and, like a mother with a child, cradled it around his nose. "Blow." And like an obedient child he blew.

Paul knew that he looked a mess, and he was even

more ashamed at the thought that he was red-eyed and tear-stained and haggard, and he could feel Mathilde's hand moist against his cheek. Hardly a way to win back a woman's heart, especially a woman like Mathilde. What if all her former swains returned with whimpers on their lips and tears in their eyes: something for her to look forward to with great expectations!

"And what are you up to these days?" Paul asked, lifting his head. She settled back on the sofa, still holding his hand but separated physically now from him by only a couple of feet — to Paul it seemed like miles. But she could still read him like a book, for as she repeated the question, almost dreamily, she made a sign for him to come closer, which he did, nestling his head on her shoulder.

"Pretty much the same old thing," she said. "I interview and pick the models for several fashion houses. I also book them into foreign houses for their showings. Not much different from when we were together."

"In those days I had a feeling you weren't doing a damn thing," Paul said with great conviction.

She laughed. "You're right," she admitted. "There was always someone to pay my rent or my basic frivolities. And now, when I desperately need the help, the competition is getting tougher by the day."

"What's this 'desperate need' you're referring to? Don't tell me you have the slightest problem finding anyone you want to. . . ."

"First of all, darling, I have a lot harder time than you, with your rose-colored glasses that are ten years behind the times, can imagine," she said with a warm and wonderful laugh that struck him like the chime of a clock. "And furthermore, I'm living with someone who would not, how shall I say, be delighted if he learned I was looking."

There was a moment's silence.

"You mean your Englishman? Your husband is English, no? I thought he was living in England."

"I spent a fair amount of time there when I was married. But after my divorce I took up with one of his cousins, who is far less rich and less good-looking than my husband but who is more, how shall I say . . . easier to live with. He's a man whose first priority is to make sure I'm happy, and is very discreet and undemanding. That's a very rare combination, I assure you, especially in men. And in women, too, I suspect."

Paul turned away, as if he were hurt. Had she had to tell him all that? It seemed to him both useless and in poor taste. But hold on: who was he to judge what was in poor taste as far as he and Mathilde were concerned? What place had he had in her life these past ten years that gave him the right to be offended or upset about someone else whose primary goal in life had apparently been to make her happy?

It was incredible! But at the same time he had detected in Mathilde's tone the same cynicism they both had shared when it came to talking about each other's past mistresses and lovers, which they had always discussed in a bantering way, as if each of their former conquests had been a kind of foxhunt, and they the lucky hunters, reveling in the game with not so much as a twinge of regret. But this time Mathilde had found a good and decent man. The fact remained, Paul had an innate distrust of good and decent men, as he had for high-minded idealists, intractable autocrats, fanatics of any ilk, not to mention all those of a practical bent. And as he did for all those male types he knew he could never be and was therefore quick to categorize as "artificial." Yes, you could love Mathilde despite knowing that she would inevitably give you a hard time now and then.

Now that he thought of it, she was the one who had broken off their relationship: how many more of her shenanigans could he have taken? He thought of their time together, how he was haunted by his fear of losing her, of never living up to her standards, of constantly wondering whether she was really cheating on him. Could his love have been strong enough to make him put up with anything more? But then, he thought suddenly, could he have put up with anything better? For the past eight hours he had been such a walking zombie, in such deep distress, that he believed he was ready to find happiness where he could, much as he was allergic to all destruction, and violently opposed to the reflexes and contractions of love. But in reality, what would he have done if she had been more to him than a mistress, if she had loved him without reservation and told him so? Would he have appreciated a less volatile relationship, one that was profound and stable, less dangerous than the one they had known, or would it have sent him flying out the door? Would he ever really know?

After all, wasn't it in fact Mathilde's escapades, her

madcap adventures, her crazy flights of fancy, her manifest bad faith, yes, even her disappearing acts, that had so endeared her to him? What if she had been a faithful, dutiful mate; would he still have loved her? No, probably not. Idiot that he was — and still is, he corrected himself — he had always been attracted to femmes fatales, or to little bitches. How could he have known that one day he would end up hoping and dreaming that these femmes fatales would somehow turn magically into Florence Nightingales?

Thank God that was what had actually happened — in a way, at least for the moment — with Mathilde. She had always left in her wake a bleating herd of love victims. And maybe, when push came to shove, that was all he was: one more notch in Mathilde's gun. The mere thought plunged him back into the depths of loneliness and despair, into the horror that had plagued him all day long. Like a gust of wind, he caught a whiff of the terror, the violence, the objective reality of the next six months, during which his body, despite all his efforts to the contrary, his still powerful lust for life, and despite all the efforts of modern science, was going to slowly wither away. But once again the shadow of death receded into the distance, taking with it the overriding fear it had brought with it. Or maybe it was simply the comforting presence of Mathilde that made death seem less terrifying.

Because the only way — or so it seemed to him — that you could face up to the idea of your death, of the dark pit, the "nothingness," with a certain degree of equanimity was if you felt that you had been loved, that your loss would be truly felt, that you had been admired, that your death had left a gaping hole in the lives of others. That you were someone who had been admired, someone whose life had been meaningful, someone who had meant a great deal to others, who had touched their lives. But if he, Paul, had been no more than a number on some anonymous list, if he had been an unknown, a mere shadow who had never made a deep impression on anyone, who had never made anyone's heart beat faster, if he was someone whose memory would never bring tears to the eyes of others, then that anonymity, already unbearable in life, would relegate him to a common grave wherein resided the ghosts of those who were the nobodies of this world, the insignificant ones, the "forgettables," and that made death worse than unbearable: it became humiliating, the ultimate humiliation. . . . All day long his death had seemed to him unbearable not so much because he kept seeing himself as worthless or mediocre, but because the reflecting image revealed nothing in him that was tender or necessary. Yes, that was the word: *necessary.* With the notable exception of Mathilde, who after ten years' separation had risen to the occasion, shown how attractive he still was in her eyes, and how much she had missed him, as she had also shown by her immediate, spontaneous reaction that she would stand by him through thick and thin, that in the few months he had left she would take care of him, love him, make him feel, no matter what, that he was still the "Lover" with a capital "L," the bright and shining lover, the wild and crazy Paul, who had loved her passionately and whose love she had cherished until death would them part.

It was as if all the hopes and dreams of Paul's adolescent days, which had little by little been repressed, gagged, in any event ground down by the demands and compromises of life, had suddenly come alive again, crying out to be heard in the little time he had left. And for the overly sentimental, what had been bearable in life — that long series of emotional disappointments — had turned out to be their only real scream for help, lasting from cradle to grave.

And speaking of screams, from all he'd heard you didn't hear many cries of pain and anguish these days when you were hospitalized — which was all to the good — thanks to the miracles of modern medicine, or rather to the widespread use today of painkilling drugs. Could he prove that? Well, one sure sign was that you never heard any longer about those famous "last words," the wise thoughts and precious fragments that people used to utter on their deathbeds, that people would duly note and pass on to future generations. The moribund were too drugged to talk anymore.

"Won't your Englishman be showing up sometime soon?" he said, less tentatively than he sounded, for he now felt certain where he stood with Mathilde.

He saw a thin smile flit across her lips, and for the first time felt the full impact of her undeniable charm.

"He spends Mondays and Tuesdays in London," she said.

"And will he let you take care of me? How do you think he's going to feel about that?"

"I'm fairly sure he won't have a problem. I loved you deeply enough, and vice versa — we were both enough in love — for me not to abandon you now," she said, running her fingers through his hair as if time had suddenly contracted, a caress of total confidence, which he found all the more affecting because she was in the driver's seat; he had placed himself entirely in her hands, not to mention that he was, in addition to everything else, the intruder in her life.

Man oh man, what a stroke of luck to have found Mathilde again! He who was so worried that he would never lay eyes on her again, or in the unlikely event he did, that she would refuse to see him, or if she did see him, would reject him out of hand. Her reaction — her immediate display of love and affection — was more than he could have hoped for. The thought brought a fresh rush of tears to his eyes, despite all his efforts to hold them back. But without a word Mathilde simply took the sleeve of her dressing gown and wiped them away, as if it were the most natural thing in the world for her to be drying the tears of a forty-year-old man, a macho man, a rugged, athletic loverboy who in six months would be dead.

The sofa on which they were sitting was too short to hold them comfortably, and for all this time he had had his legs tucked up under him, with his head on her shoulder, with the result that, because of the awkward position, he had developed cramps that, little by little, had transformed themselves into another, very specific reaction in another part of his anatomy.

And as if on cue, they both got to their feet and, speaking of Michelangelo, repaired to Mathilde's bedroom.

He couldn't remember whether he followed or pre-

ceded her into the bedroom, where, near the base-
board, an amber night-light was glowing, exactly as it
had ten years before in their other apartment. He un-
dressed quickly, as he had always done in their past
life, in today's bathroom, which was more tastefully
furnished than "theirs" had been, but also smaller.
There were scads and scads of beauty lotions, and
sponges of all shapes and sizes; and an endless number of framed illustrations lined the walls. He also
noted several striped bathrobes, which he sized up as
unisex. He took a quick shower, then banged himself
as he emerged from the shower, which like the bathroom itself was much less spacious than their shower
had been in the old apartment on the rue Bellechasse.

In fact, this whole apartment was considerably
smaller than "theirs" had been. No less charming, but
more confining. He looked for a male dressing gown
on her shelves, where, he recalled, she used to keep
them, and found none. The one hanging on the wall
was clearly hers, he surmised, since he noticed a spot
of her makeup on the inside collar. Which meant that
her Englishman brought his own dressing gown when
he came calling. Which therefore meant Mathilde was
telling him the truth when she said there were no
other men in her life but the Brit. Since she was endowed with a rare combination of thoughtfulness on
the one hand and cynicism on the other, he knew she
would have had an extra male dressing gown — and
probably a new toothbrush — somewhere on the
premises for the potential unexpected overnight guest.
When the Englishman had arrived in her life he had
doubtless eliminated those niceties exactly as Paul had

done ten years before. At the height of their affair, when they literally couldn't keep their hands off each other, the very notion of another person in either of their lives was unthinkable. That had lasted a year: a blessed year, the memory of which came flooding back to him now as he felt her warm and tender lips caressing his forehead, as he remembered her dressing-gown collar, slightly stained, as, in all likelihood, her life was; stained as his life too had been throughout the day, as he had carried with him the gnawing, growing thought of death, as he sought in vain for someone, anyone, who would rise up and curse God, rail against the medical profession, and who, whether they resorted to tea leaves or tarot cards or some quack they had heard of or read about, would say a resounding "no" to his death. No one had cried out in protest against his death; but then, hadn't he been the first to accept it, to announce it as if it were an accomplished fact? Who would dare, who (besides that bastard Gaubert) would even say, or pretend, that it couldn't be true?

He was seated on the edge of the bathtub, his hands on his knees. All he wanted was to give vent to his tears in Mathilde's arms; she would know how to deal with his grief. A natural, animal-like, instinctive grief. A grief that was almost sensual. And for some strange reason he related it to a film he had once seen, a jungle picture, in which a boy had befriended a monkey — or was it an ape? — anyway they had grown up together, and the monkey was dying, and the boy was holding the monkey in his arms, and you could see by the way they were looking at each other that they loved each other, their feelings transcending the fact that they were of different species, and the boy was "talking" to his friend, not in words but with grunts and cries, and tears were streaming down his cheeks, and death came to the jungle creature with boy and monkey holding hands. And then the boy turned in a rage and smote the man who had killed his monkey friend. Tenderness and rage combined, that was Mathilde. She would do anything for him. She would be with him, in body and in spirit, to the bitter end. It would be she who would close his eyes when it was all over. And then, having performed that final task, she would rise up in wrath against the doctor who had made him suffer, or who had allowed him to suffer. Unless of course she returned, having done her duty, to her Englishman. But Mathilde did love him, of that he was sure. She would stick by him no matter what, would not shy away from any task, however difficult or even repugnant. He imagined the last image of his life, folded in Mathilde's arms.

But she would probably get over his death more quickly than Helen. Helen, he knew, was not up to taking care of him, she would shake her head and say that she couldn't bear to see him waste away, couldn't, just couldn't stand to remember him that way; and if anyone questioned her motives she would sigh and say it was "out of respect for him," that she owed it to his pride, his virility, his God knows what. He could not picture Helen passing him the bedpan, for example. Not her style. But then, he had to admit, that thought turned him off, too (ah, yes, he really had to track down that hunting rifle, no question about it!). The same hypocrisy would obtain for Sonia, too, he knew. He could just hear her going on (to whom?) about how she couldn't, no, she really couldn't, bear to "see her dear, darling man, her great big loverboy, in *that* condition!" She loved him too much, loved him too much *physically* if you must know, to ruin all her happy memories of their times together. Especially their times in bed together. "But it wasn't only that, doctor, there were so many other things too . . ." he could hear her saying.

Thank God for Mathilde, whom he had loved as he had loved no one else in his life. Mathilde . . . who had also made him suffer as no one else ever had. And here he was slipping into bed beside her — into this vast, unknown continent of a bed, unknown that is except for the lingering odor of her perfume, which was still the same — slipping into her arms, taking the whole weight of the present with him. He lay there without moving, somehow completely at peace but also devoid of all desire, yet feeling no shame whatsoever for his state of flaccid tranquillity; all of which seemed to suit Mathilde just fine: she wrapped her arms around him, around his torso and neck, virtually lashing him to her, and when their knees touched and her legs found his, she bent them just enough so that they fit perfectly. Their faces were also touching, not in a kiss but cheek to cheek, and he felt her peaceful hand gently in his hair. That maternal hand, of whose persuasive power he had had ample proof, which was now making no effort to remind him of its ardent qualities or to rouse him from this strange state of paralysis. Especially strange, in fact, because for ten years he had been searching for and dreaming of this moment . . . And his inertia did not stem from the fact that her hips were a little fuller now, her breasts slightly less firm, her neck a trifle less swanlike. All of which would on the contrary have aroused him. In fact, under any other circumstances he would have spent hours caressing this less-seductive neck, these new folds of flesh, these defenseless breasts, these motherly hips — she had never been a mother, he suddenly realized, precisely because of the men in her life; all these men-children, all these self-centered adolescents, whom she had nurtured and pampered and turned into adults — too quickly for most of them, who would have preferred to remain under her loving protection — all these men who were on the one hand suffering from a mother-complex and on the other uncertain of their sexuality, all these young men who had paraded through her life and done their damnedest to avoid growing up. She had never had the time — or perhaps made the effort — to transform any of her lovers into fathers.

Paul understood all these things dimly and confusedly as he lay there in Mathilde's arms, in the protective embrace of Mathilde, in the warmth and energy of Mathilde, in her devotion to and affection for him. That night of rediscovery, that romantic, violent, sensual night with its confessions and explanations and tears and sighs — everything he had imagined as the only excuse for his former suffering — ended thus, to Paul's great regret. Just that. Nothing more. She, his ex-mistress, filled with an undeniable tenderness for him, he enveloped in a feeling of complete confidence

in her — the woman who had dropped him. The up-
shot, or the moral, of their story became confused,
like everything else. Paul stopped trying to figure it
out and fell asleep. He thought he was dreaming, and
in fact he was, and he believed he was enjoying his
dream. He thought he was in love with a woman he
had never seen before. He thought he had fainted and
died in a hospital bed. He thought he was very young
and in the best of health. He thought that someone he
cared about very much was shaking his shoulder. And
this last dream was real: Mathilde, who was propped
up on her elbows, was holding his face firmly in her
left hand and smothering his neck, his chin, his right
cheek with tiny, tender kisses. It was dark outside.

"Darling, it's nine o'clock," she whispered. "You
can go back to sleep if you like, but I thought I heard
you mention you had to go somewhere to dinner at
nine o'clock."

He smiled, sat up, kissed her shoulder, and made
no reference to the innocence of their encounter. It
was all too obvious. Unless, of course, he were to
drop dead in the street or be rushed howling to the
hospital emergency room or commit suicide within
the hour or leave without Mathilde for parts unknown . . .

"I'd like you . . . I want you to go away with me.
Somewhere. Maybe to the country. Any old place.
You pick it."

"That's fine with me," she said blithely. "I'd love
to. All I ask is that you give me a couple of days' notice — whether it's Helsinki or North Africa — so I
know what clothes to pack."

"And what about your Brit?" he said without looking at her.

He was knotting his tie, his back to her, registering without really seeing some tiny signs of her straitened circumstances. Maybe so, but she had a devoted man in her life. Someone who cared and shared. Yes, shared: that was the key word. For instance, that bulky blue-and-green sweater hanging over there: was it Mathilde's or the Englishman's? And what about that framed photograph of a country house? He'd never seen that before. And that crumpled raincoat: his or hers? "Theirs," was the answer. It was all "theirs." Whereas he . . . he who was paying rent for two apartments had nothing in either he could call his own. So what if he had paid for it? That didn't mean it was his. Whether it was Sonia's or Helen's, the world would be quick to recognize that everything in either place belonged not to him but to one of them. Her taste. Her property, in the eyes of society and the law.

"And what about your English friend?" he said again. "Do you really think he'll agree to this arrangement?"

"I can't say he'll be overjoyed," she said slowly, "but he loves me. And he knows that I love him, as he's also aware that I loved you deeply. . . . No . . . no, now that I think about it, I suspect it's best to keep him in the dark as long as possible," she said evenly, turning to face him. "The whole truth and nothing but the truth was never exactly the idol we worshiped, was it?"

She burst out laughing, and suddenly Paul remembered with absolute clarity the early days of their love.

The images were for some reason in black and white. They were both involved with someone else, and they were both trying to figure out how they could break off the relationships and be together. They were walking along the rue de Varenne, near the Rodin Museum, for their clandestine rendezvous point had been behind Rodin's sculpture "The Kiss," and they had both agreed that when they told their partners of the moment that it was all over it was essential they do so with elegance and grace. But they had still not made love — precisely because they were still attached — and each time they met next to Rodin's "The Kiss" their desire increased severalfold. Which struck him in retrospect as a bit strange, since the sculpture itself was probity and decency incarnate. Yet it was nonetheless arousing. . . . But then, he thought to himself, what didn't arouse them both in those days, in the first flush of their desire? A desire that both of them saw — to their amazement, fear, and utter delight — turning into love. Yes, Rodin's "The Kiss," so formal and yet so passionate.

"Do you remember our statue?" he said. "He is seated, so is she, I forget the exact setting. He is leaning over her, his hand on her hip. Her head is thrown back, yet at the same time is straining upward toward him: she is already somewhere else. Mathilde . . ."

Once again she allowed Rodin to influence her private life. She looked up at Paul's face, he for whom she meant everything, he for whom she no longer meant anything. She let him compare her to his young mistresses, to her disadvantage or to his, with all the sadness and tender indifference that you can feel for someone who is going to die and whom you no longer love. As for Paul, he wondered — and took no pleasure in the thought — whether Mathilde's face had always been as coarse and poetic at the same time. The thought gave him no pleasure, but he did not find it amusing, and it filled him with tenderness.

IX

CONTRARY TO HIS INGRAINED HABITS as an adulterer or a man-who-was-always-late, Paul rang his own doorbell, the intention being to surprise Helen, thereby, or so he hoped, putting the bug in her ear that all was not well, the purpose being to make his own task easier. It was not every day you had to inform your wife of her impending widowhood.

For some strange reason, he had serious qualms of conscience, not to mention considerable remorse, about telling this woman, who did not love him and had told him so, the awful truth. This said, he could not help thinking that his ringing his own doorbell was as odd and incomprehensible as his odd notion of showing up at Sonia's with his arms laden with chrysanthemums.

Looking at it another, more practical way, how-ever, all he was doing was giving her back the keys to her apartment. Nothing inside this place was his — with the exception of the bills, of course — and that included the absolutely useless smoking-room desk that she had had her decorator boyfriends install, as well as his own bedroom, which was separated from Helen's by not one but two bathrooms. He had never felt at home here anyway, at least not any more than he had in a nondescript hotel room; all of which didn't matter when all was said and done, because the only places he ever had felt at home were other people's houses: not that many "other people," but there were some who had loved him a lot, or more than most, or differently. You could count the places on the fingers of one hand: his parents' house, his grandmother's, his room on the rue Colbert when he had been an architect student (the first room he had found and paid for himself). And of course Mathilde's apartment, which for quite a while had given him the impression that he was living on the edge of a volcano but one that was rumbling for him and him alone. How wrong he had been.

Meanwhile, he definitely did not feel at home in this apartment, but that was something he'd never tell Helen. In fact, he would not say a word to Helen tonight about today's news. Tomorrow maybe, if he could bring himself to. Tomorrow morning or tomorrow evening. Today he was still in too confused a state, his feelings were too mixed up and unclear, he was liable to make no sense whatsoever. If he had opened his big mouth earlier in the day, rack it up to chance and chance alone. Well, chance and fatigue.

Helen opened the door to reveal a face that was — how could he describe it? — resolute, and a décolleté evening dress that told him (a) they were dining out tonight and (b) he was very late. Instinctively he glanced at his watch: it was not only after nine o'clock, it was, truth to tell, a quarter to ten.

"You're late," Helen said as if to confirm the obvious. Fatigue, disdain, regret, and reproach fought for the upper hand in her voice; her full array of vocal arms, whose intent was to overwhelm and submerge him, which she managed to do most of the time with a fair degree of success.

"Oh, no, not today!" thought Paul, suddenly freed from any feeling of guilt. Tough titty: so she'll learn of her impending widowhood a trifle earlier than planned. But it's her own fault. The problem with Helen was that she had no notion of how moody she was, or in fact that she even had moods. Her inner life required a plot, generally in two acts, and the moral of the story had to be made eminently clear, so that she could lay the blame or, on the contrary, decide in favor of her protagonist. That is, lay blame on him and decide in favor of herself. Before she could put her conflicts behind her, it was necessary for her to settle them once and for all.

"Not all that late," he said. "I'm not really *that* late."

"Why, did you accept another dinner?" she said. "I told you we were invited tonight to the Jackys', and furthermore I reminded you it was an invitation we had accepted three weeks ago. An invitation for nine o'clock. To make things worse, I ran into Elaine Jacky the day before yesterday and she left me saying, 'See you on the twelfth!'"

"And is today the twelfth?" Paul asked, suddenly interested. "What's today? Thursday?"

"Today's *Tuesday* the twelfth," she corrected him,

after having seemed for a moment to be taken aback by his question. "Why? Did you schedule another dinner?"

"No, but tomorrow would have been Friday the thirteenth, and I would have found that amusing," he responded, sitting down on the hallway bench — the spot where their mutual antipathy had stopped them. His initial compassion to spare her the news had vanished the moment she had reminded him of dinner at the Jackys', which was already hard to take when he was in good health.

"Listen, I have to talk to you. Cancel that dinner."

"You mean what you have to discuss is important enough to justify our unforgivable rudeness? Am I supposed to believe that?"

She had nonetheless grown pale as she said those words. She was trying to pinpoint what specifically would have made him say that. Not the real reason, of course, something else. Maybe divorce. Was it possible, considering how absurd their life was together, that she really didn't want to let him go? Did she still care about him? A whole series of vain questions rushed forward and made their bows and curtsies before the throne of his pride but with an absence of charm and warmth that made Paul banish them without further ado.

"No," he said. "That is, yes. I'm sure this dinner is of no importance. This morning I went to see . . . what's his name, the hamster who is Dr. Jouffroy's replacement?"

She looked at him more closely now, clearly concerned. It was true that she had never laid eyes on Dr.

Jouffroy, in fact barely knew who he was, since Paul's robust good health was taken for granted by their friends and acquaintances. No one would ever have said, or even thought: "Paul doesn't look well today." Well, he had news for them. Bad news. Or maybe good, depending on how they really felt about him.

"My doctor," said Paul. "My doctor gave me a whole battery of tests, including CAT scans, and to make a long story short I've got this lousy thing on my lungs and I'm going to die a lot sooner than expected."

Somehow he couldn't bring himself to say, "Six months. I've got six months to live." The fact was, he was more afraid of her reaction than he was of that of the other two women in his life who loved him, or at least claimed to. As if she, the beautiful Helen, was more fragile than the others. Helen the sadist, the proud, and the puritan. When all was said and done, she was the one he worried about the most, as if in fact her indifference, her pride, had stripped her of any protective armor, the armor that protects the vulnerable of this world and allows them to give vent to their feelings by crying their hearts out, sobbing or gnashing their teeth in the face of the inadmissible horror of the death of a loved one. Helen had never suffered anything but appropriate grief, that is to say grief brought about by the appropriate next of kin or friends — assuming of course that grief can ever be appropriate. One was an uncle whose head had been more in the clouds than focused on his business, who went bankrupt and shortly thereafter — probably as a direct result — suffered a heart attack; another was one of her fellow students in college, who was as enormously talented as she was mean-spirited and, unable to bear the mediocrity of her existence, decided to cut it short; still another was one of her ardent suitors, whose speed to win her heart was matched only by his speed on the highway, with disastrous results. In other words, grief that she could allow herself to indulge in and feel good about, both in public and in private. But when it came to Paul, the unfaithful husband, the pathological liar, the intimate stranger whom she thought she had loved, blinded as she was by his youth and charm, how was she going to handle that? Of course, in the eyes of the world she would be an admirable widow, self-controlled, proper, a widow with great poise and perfect taste. But once she was by herself, away from the eyes of the world, when she had to deal with the low blows of memory, the songs they had heard together, the impassioned, carefree times they had shared — all those happy moments that nonetheless constituted a fair portion of their life together and that she would do her best to erase from her mind, how was she going to deal with those? Which of her "dear friends" — either the snobs or the slaves or the two combined — could she call at four in the morning to moan or groan or complain to her heart's content? She'd find someone she could turn to, someone who "would understand her grief," as her right-thinking friends would put it.

She came over to him. "I'm here, you know. I'm here," she said, and she laid her hand on his lapel.

The look she gave him — full of devotion and compassion and pain — sent a shiver up his spine. Paul sat down suddenly on the sofa. Yes, no question about it: she, like the others, had no trouble imagining him dead. Women believed in death. Without exception. It was part of their makeup. Whereas men refused to face up to it. Not only death, in fact, but life, too: a man, learning that his wife or girlfriend is pregnant, reacts like some beast of the field — "I can't believe it's true!" — while women look at the same situation as either happy news or a momentary inconvenience.

Helen was sitting next to him on the sofa, staring at him intently. She ran her fingers slowly through his hair. He could smell her perfume, and that plus the touch of her hand he found upsetting, but also arousing. And then he had a vulgar reaction that wasn't really like him, and he thought to himself: "My God, if this keeps up, the combination of keeping Mathilde and Sonia and Helen happy all the time is going to be the death of me yet!" and he had to turn his face away so that Helen would not see the ironic smile on his lips.

"I'll help you," she said, "with all the strength I have. For starters, I'm going to cancel my trip."

"What trip?"

"The trip I was planning to take with Philip. But knowing what I now know, there's no way in the world I could leave you. I'll explain to Philip what's happened. He'll understand. And if he doesn't, that's his tough luck."

"Ah, yes, that's true ," he said. "You two were taking a trip together. Or was it a cruise? It somehow slipped my mind."

Philip Guérand was in the diplomatic service, and a very proper fellow indeed. So proper in fact that Paul regularly forgot his existence, which was that of one more poor bastard in the life of his wife. But of course they should go off together as planned. It would be silly of them not to take this trip, or cruise, or whatever it was. It could be their trial honeymoon.

"I insist that you keep to your plans," Paul said. "I'm told I'll be fine for the next three or four months. So I don't need anyone's help right now."

"But of course you do, silly boy. Even if you refuse to face up to it yet, if this new circumstance hasn't yet become a reality for you, you do need someone. What is marriage all about anyway?"

He looked at her and read in her eyes a kind of excitement, a kind of new drive or energy that completely turned him off.

"Because you married me for better or for worse, is that what you're referring to?" he said.

Whatever she may think consciously, some part of her inner self is delighted. The inner self that has been waiting for this moment for eight years now. He pictured himself dying in this lugubrious apartment, cared for by a qualified nurse, his wife surrounded by a number of her female friends, all patting her hand and telling her how sorry, how terribly sorry, they are. And the same picture was completely devoid of any of his own friends, all of whom had been denied entrance by his grieving wife. In fact, he saw nothing in the picture but loneliness, sadness, dejection, as he moved slowly, implacably, obediently toward death. Oh, Mathilde! Mathilde! How could he have had a moment's hesitation about intruding in her life? Sonia was no longer even a remote possibility in his mental landscape. Gone. Over. Done with. Sonia knew Helen, and when she talked about her she either sounded like the little slut she was or she took on grand airs.

The other question was: could he really manage to evade Helen's clutches? The simple, heartfelt response, provided by Mathilde, came back to him: "I'll take care of you." Even Helen was no match for Mathilde's quiet energy, her commanding presence. He might die in the small, three-room apartment on the rue de Tournon, but he would die pampered and loved. He'd give Mathilde enough money so that she could quit the thankless job that took so much out of her and bored her to tears. He should have told her that right off the bat. The fact that at thirty-five she had been footloose and fancy-free and didn't give a damn about money or security didn't mean that at forty-five financial matters shouldn't be taken care of, especially since this Englishman of hers seemed to have his head in the clouds and a profession that didn't exactly spell security. Of course, he should have realized it sooner: Mathilde was probably already short of money, which explained why the collar of her dressing gown had a spot on it. She probably couldn't even afford to pay for dry cleaning! Yes, that had to be it: he remembered that when they were together he had always made sure she had enough to pay for such things, since whatever else he was he was a stickler for cleanliness. He would withdraw the necessary funds from his firm tomorrow. He would show up at her apartment, check in hand, to make sure all her wants and needs were taken care of. He would provide her with something besides love, which she could use to good advantage. Which would last her after love was gone. No need for any further romantic posturing in bed, which only upset him. She was a woman of discriminating taste, and would understand his gesture. And anyway, in two or three months he would not be making love to her. So fast, so far, so impossible, so irrevocable . . .

"I have to make a phone call," he said.

But Helen held him back. "I have to call the Jackys first," she said, "and offer our apologies. Then I'll make us some soup and spaghetti if you're too tired to go out for dinner."

There was something formidable about the way she stressed the word "us." And he got to his feet.

"Don't bother," he said. "I want you to run off to the Jackys' and make my excuses. No, no excuses: just tell them the thought of having dinner with them was more than I could bear. And don't wait up for me, Helen. . . . And there's one other thing: I forbid you to cancel your trip with Philip."

And then, with a final effort to dredge up the poor man's full name, and as a final act of courtesy, he blurted, "Philip Guérand, right? There's no reason he ought to sit on his hands for years waiting for you."

"Because you're off to sleep with one of your sluts, is that it?" Helen said, furious now. "It doesn't matter what state you're in. Even if you can't . . . even if you're entirely incapable of . . . you still . . ."

From the next room, the phone rang imperiously.

"It has to be the Jackys," she said, "wondering what's happened to us."

"They probably want to tell you the soufflé's just fallen flat," he said pleasantly.

Helen was not amused. She gave him an icy glance and went into the living room. Paul slipped on his coat and checked to make sure he had his keys.

"It's for you," Helen said, emerging from the living room.

He walked over and picked up the phone. It took him a second to recognize the nasal voice of the hamster. The hamster! Jesus, that was all he needed to make his day complete! Dr. Creep must have set up some appointments for him with his esteemed medical specialists. News of Paul's superb, full-blooming carcinoma must have already made the rounds of the Paris hospitals, so that the best and brightest could bid on it. . . . How much am I bid for Paul Cazavel? The man with six months to live! Going once, going twice! . . . At dinner, the kids of the top doctors in their respective fields would pray to God that He entrust this cancer patient to the care of their dear dad. . . .

The hamster's voice seemed less smug, less self-assured than it had been this morning. And if Paul understood correctly, he seemed to be mumbling some sort of excuse, though he couldn't tell for what.

"Dr. Jouffroy, you know, whatever his other

qualities — which as you know are many — but I must say orderliness is not among them, if you don't mind my saying . . ."

What in God's name was he going on about?

"Not to mention the inexcusable carelessness of certain laboratories, which if I may say so is unforgivable. No, worse than unforgivable . . . What I'm trying to say is that I hope your day hasn't been too upsetting, that you haven't been dwelling too much on what I told you this morning. . . ."

"Will you get to the goddamn point?"

"It's simply that there was an error. A grave error, I'm afraid. Your tests were, I'm sorry to say, mixed up with somebody else's. . . ."

Paul was overcome with a rage so total, so complete, that there was no room for any feeling of relief.

"Dr. Hamster," he said icily, "do you have the *slightest* idea what your 'error' has caused me? Do you have any idea whatsoever? Apparently you don't even know how to read an X-ray properly, not to mention a CAT scan. Or any other medical report either, I'm sure, Dr. Hamster. . . . What? That's not your name? What the hell do I care what your goddamn name is, Dr. Hamster? To me that's your name. And the first thing I'm going to do is apologize to all hamsters. I'm going to pretend I never heard of you, and I strongly suggest you do the same about me. Oh, and one other thing. Go fuck yourself."

He slammed down the phone, trembling with rage and joy.

He must have been yelling, because from the next room he heard a discreet cough. Helen's discreet cough, emanating from a thoroughly frightened woman.

He decided to exit the apartment by the kitchen door. He was going to rent a room in that charming old hotel on the rue Fleurus where he hadn't been for several months now. And there he would fling himself across his bed and fall asleep, fully clothed, without a woman, without a hamster. And without cancer.

He felt his entire being slowly filling with something that he knew was happiness. Something triumphant and modest at the same time. He got up from his chair and found that he had trouble walking steadily, trouble keeping his balance. It was the first time, he said to himself as he tiptoed across the kitchen, it was indeed the first time in his life that solitude was making him drunk. . . .